MURDER EN SUITE

A JOYCE AND GINGER MYSTERY

KATE P ADAMS

ALSO BY KATE P ADAMS

THE CHARLETON HOUSE MYSTERIES

Death by Dark Roast

A Killer Wedding

Sleep Like the Dead

A Deadly Ride

Mulled Wine and Murder

A Tragic Act

A Capital Crime

Tales from Charleton House

THE JOYCE AND GINGER MYSTERIES

Murder En Suite

For
Joanna Hancox & Becki Scott,
with love

'What I still don't understand is why we're staying in a hotel so close to our homes. We could just go for dinner, prop up the bar for a few hours, then I could get a taxi back to the comfort of my own bed. This seems like a rather pointless exercise to me.'

Joyce looked over at Ginger with a weary expression. They'd often talked about having a girls' weekend away together, but Joyce had meant heading down to London, or perhaps jumping on the Eurostar and enjoying the charms of Parisian men as they dined on a bateau-mouche with the Eiffel Tower above them. Not driving half an hour down the road from where she worked and staying in a town she knew like the back of her hand. Like the back of both hands and both her feet, come to think of it.

'Because, my dear, you don't have to make the bed in the morning. Because you don't have to make your own coffee, you can have breakfast brought to your room. Because there will be an entire cocktail bar at our disposal, and because my good friend is the manager of the hotel and he's invited me to stay for free and I've had the good heart to invite you along as my plus one. Although I can drop you off at a bus stop and go on my own if you'd prefer.' Ginger started to indicate and slow the car down as they neared a concrete box of a bus station up ahead.

Joyce wasn't up for a bus ride. 'There is something seriously wrong with the world the day I get on a smelly, germ-ridden tin can. I'm assuming we get a room each? I imagine you're a snorer.'

Ginger crunched through the gears as she increased the speed again. 'Of course.' It didn't escape Joyce's notice that Ginger didn't seem entirely confident in her response, but Joyce wasn't planning on accepting anything less than her own room. She could always deal with that at reception.

Joyce hadn't known Ginger for very long. The two single women, both in their late sixties, had met the previous year and over numerous glasses of champagne had discovered that despite being wildly different in almost every way, they made good, if rather odd, friends. Ginger, a sturdy woman who repaired her own garden walls and refused to buy clothing that had special washing requirements (silk being an exception to the rule), and Joyce, who spent more time over her makeup each morning than Ginger spent in a typical year, had found in one another comfortable companions. Conversation had quickly turned to weekends away, but with spa breaks being Joyce's preferred choice, while a weekend tramping over the mountains of the Lake District or exploring the history of a city with a guide book in one hand formed the basis of Ginger's suggestions, time had flown and nothing had come of the plans. Until Joyce got a phone call.

'Pack up your lipsticks, unplug your hair straighteners, and get ready to relax. We have an all-expenses-paid weekend in a newly renovated hotel with an excellent cocktail bar.' Joyce hadn't questioned the free aspect of it; she was all in. She just hadn't expected her dreams of Monaco or Vegas to be interrupted with, 'We're off to Buxton.'

'Buxton?' she had screeched. Even Joyce had to admit that it was a screech. 'I do my shopping in Buxton. If I need to go inside an actual bank, I go to Buxton. I do not go to Buxton for a weekend of glamour and relaxation.'

'We've always talked about going away together. If it turns out that we drive each other up the wall, this is a whole lot easier than trying to avoid each other for a weekend when we're somewhere like Madrid, and then having to sit next to each other on the plane home, fighting wordlessly over the arm rest. Glamour is all in the mind, love, it's all in the mind.'

'It's all in your bloomin' mind if you think I'm coming,' Joyce had muttered.

'I heard that, you ungrateful madam. I'll pick you up from work next Friday at 4pm.'

'We don't close the shop until six.'

'You're the boss. Get someone else to do it.'

Joyce couldn't argue with that. She was in charge and never shied away from delegating if she needed to pop out to buy a new pair of shoes ("need" being a relative word; she owned over 200 pairs) or her favourite mascara was running low.

'Alright,' she'd grumbled. 'Only I'm not going up any bloody hills for one of your afternoon rambles.'

Joyce now looked across at Ginger. 'You better be right about the extensive cocktail bar. Alcohol might be the only interesting thing about this weekend.'

Ginger brushed her rather wild and undisciplined grey hair out of her eyes, and Joyce was left distinctly uncomfortable by the smirk she was convinced she had seen flit across her friend's face. She sank into the seat for the remaining fifteen minutes' drive and closed her eyes, clinging on to the vision of a yacht bobbing in the waters of St Tropez. Dreading whatever reality waited for her up the road, she was going to take every available minute to indulge in her dreams.

In truth, Joyce had always been fond of Buxton, one of

England's finest Georgian spa towns. Perhaps not quite as well-known as Bath, it is still a tourist destination, flocked to by lovers of Austen and Brontë who like to imagine Mr Darcy popping by to enjoy the healing properties of the famous thermal waters. That was something that Joyce could relate to; she could easily view herself among the wealthy visitors of the 18th century. Of course, running into Mr Darcy also featured in her imaginings. He would invite her to a ball, and later accompany her to a salon or some theatrical entertainment at the Opera House, which would likely result in more racy memories than her recent visit with Ginger. After watching a rather fine Gilbert and Sullivan, Joyce had been subjected to Ginger's high-pitched declaration that she was a *Modern Major General* for the entire drive home and it had taken all her willpower not to steer them under an oncoming bus.

It had never crossed Joyce's mind to stay in Buxton itself, no matter how late some of the events she had attended finished. She would just call a taxi and enjoy the silk sheets of her own queen-sized orthopaedic alpaca-hair mattress, knowing that she could drink her favourite coffee and luxuriate in her favourite bath salts the following morning. Having said that, she did quite like the idea of a change of scenery. The gloom of January and February had started to seep into her bones. She'd managed a week on the island of Majorca at the start of the year, but the vitamin D boost she'd received had long since dwindled, and she'd resorted to pulling out the brightest of her clothes from her comprehensive wardrobe. Her yellow twinset with stylish black edging and buttons and a matching skirt had resulted in one particularly annoying colleague referring to her as a bumble bee, and her rainbow-striped woollen dress had the same cretin asking her if a pot of gold could be found under its pleats. The sniggers and range of innuendos had lasted the rest of the week. But if nature was not feeling duty bound to liven up the monochrome weather that had been blanketing the hills of Derbyshire, Joyce was more than equipped to do the job.

Now, however, she wanted a break. She hoped she possessed enough imagination to pretend that the hotel they were heading for was actually on New York's Fifth Avenue, if you ignored the northern English accents and the popularity of sausage rolls and fried breakfasts in the surrounding cafés.

Joyce's eyes popped open as she heard the squeal of tyres and the sound of Ginger shouting at another driver, informing him in rather crass tones what he could do with his Porsche SUV and where she was convinced it might fit. Joyce sank further down in her seat. It was bad enough that she had to be driven in a scratched, dented and muddy twenty-year-old three-door Ford Fiesta, her own convertible BMW currently undergoing repairs after Joyce had become a little too intimate with a wall so low it had almost been invisible, but now the language being tossed out of the window made the whole scenario more embarrassing than she thought possible. Once the driver of the SUV realised that Ginger was unlikely to be concerned about her car getting a few extra dents in a parking tussle, he drove off with a hand gesture which Joyce was sure couldn't be found in the dictionary of British Sign Language, and Ginger did a neat little reverse park into a space within sight of the front doors of The Lodge, their home for the weekend.

Joyce took a deep breath. *Imagine it's New York, imagine it's Paris,* she chanted to herself as her cherry-red lips formed a tight smile. She quickly checked her blonde hair to make sure the modern take on a beehive hadn't been damaged on the journey, convinced herself her makeup didn't need reapplying (unlikely – she'd done that thirty minutes ago), and then swung her rather impressively shapely legs out of the car. This might not be her dream destination, but she was going to make an entrance that told the staff what kind of weekend she was expecting.

$\mathcal{G}$inger looked up at the entrance with pride. She felt a bond with The Lodge, having watched it grow from a large, well-respected, but slightly tired establishment into one of the most talked-about boutique hotels in the area. The Lodge was formed from a row of Victorian villas that looked out across the Pavilion Gardens, the final touches being added during a long-term renovation programme on the top floor which had left half the rooms closed over the winter. She had contributed to the work by making a number of curtains and cushions out of a fabric that the manager had found on his travels to India and Istanbul. Ginger's career as a seamstress had seen her making ornate costumes for West End musicals, so this had been a quick and easy job for a childhood friend.

With a large holdall slung over one shoulder and a bundle containing her coat, an extra cardigan which she'd thrown in the car at the last minute, two scarves and a pair of sheepskin gloves, Ginger leant her shoulder against the door and pushed her way through. The lobby immediately sucked visitors into its warm embrace, the mahogany reception desk taking centre stage against a backdrop of dark-green walls. Contemporary artwork threw cooler colours and light into the room, each in elaborate gold frames. Two armchairs in gold fabric flanked a low table made from the stump of a tree, upturned so the roots carefully held a glass top, with flecks of gold scattered within the glass. The flamboyance of the space matched the personality of the family who owned the hotel.

Ginger heard 'Thanks' muttered from behind her, at which point she realised she had forgotten to hold the door open for Joyce, who was lugging an enormous lurid-pink suitcase behind her. Ginger might have guessed that she would have packed multiple outfit changes for each day.

'Oops, sorry, love. You alright?'

'Of course I'm alright. It…'

Ginger didn't catch the rest. She dropped the pile of clothes onto an armchair and threw her arms around the neck of a mountain of a man. Dennis Matty, the general manager and the latest of the generations of his family to run the hotel, was almost as broad as he was tall, and he was very tall. His impressive girth was clad in a beautifully tailored navy-blue pinstripe suit and deep pink tie, an outfit that Ginger could have described before she entered the building. It was his uniform of sorts; he had a wardrobe full of navy pinstripe suits and a vast collection of pink ties. Whether it was a shade of plain pink, had dots, stripes, or some other pink detail, each and every tie had a matching hand-kerchief which protruded from the breast pocket in a perfectly twisted triangle.

He gave Ginger a tight squeeze and lifted her briefly from the floor.

'Careful there, you'll do your back in.' Ginger laughed, although she wasn't kidding; she wasn't small herself. Whenever she was with Dennis, she felt like the teenager she, and he, had been when they first met.

'Never, you're as light as a feather.'

There was a soft snort and they turned together towards the door.

'I'm sorry, Dennis, this is Joyce Brocklehurst. Joyce, this is Dennis Matty.'

Dennis stepped past Ginger and took Joyce's hand in both of his, briefly examining the bright pink talons on the end of each finger. Ginger noted Joyce's appraisal of his appearance; she seemed satisfied. Dennis too seemed rather pleased with the vision before him. A dark-pink long-sleeved t-shirt with thick black and white swirls was topped off by a long pink coat. Black trousers which were a little too tight, pink shoes and a matching handbag finished off the look.

'Welcome, Joyce, I'm so pleased that Ginger brought you with her. It's going to be a pleasure to get to know you, and I want to hear all about life working for a Duke and Duchess.' His warm baritone voice echoed in the lobby. Everything about Dennis exuded warmth and familiarity.

'Oh, I only run their gift shops, it's nothing too fancy. It's lovely to meet you too, Dennis. When Ginger suggested a weekend in your fine establishment, it didn't take a moment's thought for me to accept. I've heard so much about your hotel and the word on the street is that you're doing a rather magnificent renovation.'

Ginger smiled to herself. Joyce had turned up the intensity on her 'Lady of the Manor' act. She was all Received Pronunciation and cut-glass vowels when she wanted to be, but she was a Derbyshire lass really, although the overworked enunciation didn't appear entirely out of place. With her sharp posture, chin up, designer handbag dangling from an arm held at a neat 90 degree angle and the whole display balanced on a pair of stilettos that could be used to spear fish, all Joyce lacked was a tiara, and Ginger guessed she probably had a couple of those at home.

'It's not so much a renovation as a redecoration, but I'm hoping the impact is as impressive. The upper floor was the only area yet to be refreshed and we're just having a few finishing touches done before it officially reopens on Friday. However…'

Ginger gave a small clap of her hands; she knew what was coming next.

'Yes, my dear, I've made sure two of the rooms have been finished for your arrival and you're in Mary's room. Joyce is next door.'

Ginger looked across at her friend. 'Mary, Queen of Scots. I've always wanted to stay in there, it's the most decadent room.'

'She didn't actually stay here,' Dennis explained to Joyce, 'she stayed over the road at the Old Hall, but I felt that an homage was in order, and it meant I could have a lot of fun with the whole Queen theme. Do you have all your bags? I'll carry them up for you, and then you can have some lunch.'

'No you won't,' Ginger instructed. 'We can carry our own bags. You can get busy at the bar; Joyce and I will be down for cocktails as soon as we've dropped our things off.' She saw a light come on in Joyce's eyes at the mention of cocktails.

'As you wish, madam, I will go and warm up.' He walked through a door, miming the actions of shaking a cocktail high in the air. Ginger laughed.

'Come on, Lady Muck, let's go and check out our home for the weekend. Sorry you didn't get the room fit for a queen. On this occasion, you get to be the lady's maid in the room next door.'

3

---

*J*oyce breathed in the smell of fresh paint as they ascended the stairs. She wished that Dennis had opened a few more windows, but at least it was a sign that plenty of work had been going on. As the upper floor wasn't officially open to guests yet, she shouldn't be too surprised if she saw sheets still protecting carpets or plastic wrapping on furniture. They passed two young men who were on the way down the stairs, *Bennett's Family Carpenters* written on their t-shirts, and Joyce enjoyed the lingering look one of them gave her. She hadn't lost her touch.

The solid wooden banisters matched the mahogany desk, the staircase walls covered in a grey velveteen wallpaper with an ornate pattern that gave a shimmering effect. More pictures in gold frames lined the route. Once at the top floor, the wide staircase opened out onto an attractive bright landing, a large window overlooking the Pavilion Gardens opposite. The cast-iron and glass structures of the pavilion and conservatory were two of the many landmark buildings that pulled people to the pretty town. A velvet loveseat was positioned so visitors could sit and enjoy the view.

Ginger led the way, looking from behind like a washerwoman heading to the laundry with the bundle of clothes in her arms. Joyce couldn't understand why she hadn't taken the time to fold them and add them to her bag. The picture wasn't helped by the loose skirt Ginger was wearing, which was now hanging at an odd angle, one side lower than the other, or the thick oversized fleece shirt she had put on to keep the cold out, making her look bigger than she really was.

Ginger's head turned at each room to check the name. On this floor, Joyce had noticed, the rooms were not numbered, but named: the Anne Lister; the Joseph Paxton; the Josiah Wedgwood. All names of famous people who'd held associations through the ages with Buxton or who had been known to visit, although some of the links were a little tenuous. It appeared that Dennis was a man who didn't mind playing fast and loose with history in the name of drama and fun.

A housekeeper's cart sat up ahead, just before a junction in the corridor, but there was no sign of the housekeeper.

'Here we are, Mary, Queen of Scots. This is mine; you're next door in Mr Wedgewood, so to speak.' Ginger handed Joyce a key with a soft leather tag, and then tried to insert another key into her own door. 'See you in a minute.'

'Hang on just one minute, lady. I want to check out your room first, so that when I do go into mine, I'll know if I want to swap.' Joyce was joking, but enjoyed watching Ginger roll her eyes. 'Oh, come here, give me those.' She wrestled the bundle of clothes from Ginger's arms so her friend could better manage the door. 'If that cleaner hasn't reappeared once we've had a look round, we should take some extra lotions and shower gel. They never leave enough.'

The door opened into a short corridor. As soon as they walked in, they were confronted by a portrait of Mary, giving them the once-over before they went any further. A slim woman with red-gold hair and pale skin, she was standing wearing a black dress, a hand on a wooden table and long curtains behind her. The table was a distinctly orange shade, while the curtains looked as if they should have been a kind of gold, but light bouncing off them made them also appear orange.

It was this colour that had been chosen as a key feature of the room. They stepped in and were presented with a richly decorated seating area. Fat orange velvet armchairs were set against the backdrop of William Morris-style wallpaper, which made it look fussy but welcoming. A stone bust of Mary sat on the coffee table. Long orange silk curtains, reflecting the colours in the painting of Mary, framed a large window. The remaining walls were cream velveteen.

As the two women stepped further into the room, they could see how large it was. Joyce went to examine the bathroom, until her inspection was interrupted by Ginger yelping.

'Dear God!'

'What is it?' asked Joyce idly, wondering if Ginger had come face to face with a workman, or the missing cleaner had taken her by surprise. Joyce was more interested in the bathroom, which she rather liked. A roll-top bath sat in the centre of the room, the orange tiles surrounding it warming, whereas the colour in the main room was far too dark for her liking, although certainly luxurious. She had a look at the toiletries: a very nice, and expensive, locally produced brand. She was definitely going to be raiding the housekeeper's trolley and more than once.

'JOYCE! Where the hell are you?'

'What's wrong?' Joyce made her way out of the bathroom and to the hidden half of the bedroom, which was dominated by an ornate wooden four-poster bed, patterns in the wood picked out in gold. 'Just dump your stuff and we'll go next door.'

'You don't need to worry about the cleaner catching you nicking her stuff,' Ginger declared, stepping out of the way and pointing at the bed.

'Why? Oh...' Following the direction of Ginger's finger, Joyce saw a woman dressed in black lying on the sheets. She strode towards the prone figure. 'Sleeping on the job? There'll be no tip for her.'

'I think she's dead, Joyce. In fact, I'm sure she is.'

Joyce stopped suddenly, not keen to get too close to a corpse, but still she leaned over, seeing red marks lining the woman's neck.

'I'll call reception.' She picked up the phone by the bed and dialled 0.

'Hang on one minute.' Ginger sounded curious. 'That's not a cleaner's uniform. That's Mary, Queen of Scots. Oh my goodness, I made her dress. I know her.'

4

_G_inger stepped past Joyce and checked for a pulse. There wasn't one.

'How the hell do you know Mary, Queen of Scots?' asked Joyce. 'You're old, but you're not...'

'It's Caroline Clatworthy. She works here and...'

'Come on,' instructed Joyce. 'We've got to get out of here, leave the scene as undisturbed as possible. Grab your stuff... Ginger, come on!'

Ginger gave the Queen a final look before grabbing her things and following close on Joyce's heels.

'I don't understand, did she die while taking a nap?' Ginger didn't yet feel able to confront the obvious truth: however the woman had died, it wasn't by the hand of nature. 'She's not that old, so I doubt it was the strain of work. Maybe she had a heart attack and lay down as she started to feel unwell.'

'I've no idea. But I do know I need to find the bar.'

The sound of heavy footsteps pounded along the corridor, and as Joyce turned to leave, she blocked the path of a very red-faced Dennis.

'The front desk told me you found Caroline. What's wrong, is she unwell? They said she was dead, but surely she's just a bit peaky. Can we go and...' He rushed into the room and to the bedside. His ruddy cheeks went very pale, very quickly.

Ginger stood on the opposite side of the bed. 'We need to go downstairs, Dennis, there's nothing we can do.'

'Come on. We all need a strong drink.' Joyce put a pristinely manicured hand on Dennis's shoulder and gradually turned him round to face the door. Ginger followed, thinking about what needed to be done. Right now, what was most important was that they sealed off this floor. Sealed off? Closed off? She couldn't remember how it was described on the police shows she watched, and she watched a lot. She blamed the shock for her inability to remember the right word, and then thought if that was the worst of the shock, she was going to be okay.

Dennis descended the stairs in stunned silence. Reversing their roles, Ginger made him take a seat at the bar, and then went round to the other side to get him a drink.

'Should we be doing this before the police arrive?' he asked. Ginger hesitated for a moment. It might not be the most sensible thing to do, to drink right now.

'A small one will be fine. If it helps calm us all down, then we'll be of more use to the police.' She could hear Joyce calling to a member of staff and asking – or, more precisely, demanding – that they stand at the bottom of the staircase to make sure no one went up until the police arrived.

'Are there many guests staying at the moment?' Ginger asked Dennis.

'Only a few, on the ground floor and first floor. They're all regulars and don't mind all the work going on during the day. I shouldn't be here, I should be with my staff.'

'Drink this first.'

'What is it?'

'A martini.'

'Are you out of your mind? I'll be drunk when the police get here.'

Ginger looked at him knowingly. 'No, you won't. I've seen you knock back half a dozen of these and still dance a flamenco without putting a step out of place.'

Dennis nodded his agreement and took a sip. 'I need to teach you how to make a martini.'

'Who doesn't know how to make a martini?' asked Joyce, joining them. 'Can't stand them myself, but everyone has to know how to make them.'

'I can't be good at everything,' retorted Ginger. 'Drink?'

Joyce shook her head. 'It might be the first time I've ever turned down a drink, but I'll wait. Dennis, I've given your staff their instructions, which can be summed up as stay put, say nothing and do nothing. They look like they can cope with that.'

Dennis looked in the direction of the door. Two of the hotel staff were talking, both looking pale.

'Things haven't long settled down after the thefts,' he said sadly. 'They'll need my support to get through this.'

'What thefts?' Ginger asked as she returned the gin to the shelf.

'A range of items have been taken from staff and visitors just recently, but in the last couple of weeks or so, it seemed like it had stopped and morale had been improving in leaps and bounds.' Dennis took two big gulps of the poorly made martini before heading for the door. 'I can't stay here, I'll go and say nothing and do nothing with my team.'

Joyce watched him leave, and then turned to face Ginger who was pouring herself a glass of scotch.

'Who is she... was she, I mean?'

'Caroline Clatworthy? She worked here at The Lodge as a cleaner, but was also a tour guide around Buxton. She would dress as Mary, Queen of Scots and talk about her association with the town. The Queen swore by the healing properties of the spa water here, and even when she was imprisoned by Elizabeth I, she insisted on coming here. Part of the building she was held in remains – it's the Old Hall Hotel, over the road. There's a lot of interest in her, and Caroline was one of a couple of guides to dress as her. She contacted me last year and asked if I would make the dress.'

'Do you know much about her? Caroline, I mean.'

'Almost nothing. She would come for fittings, we'd talk about the hotel or what was happening in Buxton and that was it. Small talk.' There was a pause, during which time Ginger emptied her glass in one go.

'Thanks,' Joyce said.

'What for?'

'A weekend away less than half an hour's drive from my house wasn't very appealing, but you've certainly livened things up.'

'How have I livened things up? I didn't kill her.'

'True, maybe you don't deserve all the credit, but things have certainly got more interesting around here. Now put that bottle of champagne in ice. Once the police have done with us, we'll toast this Caroline woman, and you better learn how to make a martini if that's Dennis's tipple of choice. He's going to need a few.'

5

*D*etective Sergeant Colette Harnby stood in the doorway to the bar. Joyce had watched her walk up the staircase as part of the buzz of activity that had gradually taken over the hotel in the time after the body had been found. She had known that Harnby would want to talk to them eventually; the DS had been involved in a number of investigations at Charleton House, the home of the Duke and Duchess of Ravensbury and Joyce's place of employment.

As usual, DS Harnby was wearing a very smart, very boring dark skirt suit. Joyce desperately wished that she would liven it up a bit; she understood the serious nature of the woman's role, but a more colourful shirt wouldn't have gone amiss. Perhaps an eye-catching brooch; Joyce was on a mission to brighten up the world. Harnby's dark bob framed her face almost rigidly and Joyce wanted to reach out and mess it up.

'Ginger Salt and Joyce Brocklehurst.' DS Harnby looked up from her notepad. 'I thought the names were familiar, but I couldn't see why you'd be staying at a hotel so close to home, and work.'

Joyce glanced at Ginger. 'I thought the same thing.'

'So, what are you doing here? I believe you found the body – is that correct?'

Joyce stepped down from her bar stool; it didn't seem right to be perched at a bar when being quizzed by a police detective. Harnby indicated to a small, low table with chairs around it and all three of them took a seat.

'Yes, we found her,' Joyce confirmed. 'Well, I suppose Ginger did really. She was the first in the bedroom, and we're here because Ginger knows the owner and it's a free stay, which immediately makes it more relaxing, in theory. Throw in a couple of cocktails, afternoon tea at the Old Hall Hotel and a spa treatment or three, and you get the picture.'

Harnby nodded enigmatically, then got Joyce and Ginger to run through their discovery. What had they seen? Had they touched anything? Did they know the deceased?

'Never seen her before in my life,' Joyce confirmed. 'Never been in the hotel before.'

Harnby turned to Ginger, who nodded. 'I made her dress; I also saw her here a few times. I visit Dennis a lot so I'm on speaking terms with many of the staff. But I didn't get to know her particularly well. She was strangled, is that right?'

Harnby looked at Ginger. She seemed to be considering how to respond: the official, professional way, or…

'I need to have it confirmed, but yes, it certainly looks that way. Okay, I presume I can find you here if I have any more questions?'

Joyce hadn't thought about that; Ginger's room was a murder scene. Now she was here, within arm's reach of a bar and a kitchen that food would magically appear out of without her being involved, she wasn't as keen to call an end to the weekend as she thought she might have been. But she needn't have worried.

'Absolutely,' Ginger confirmed. 'There's plenty of room and I plan on sticking around to help Dennis. He's bound to need some support.'

Harnby closed her notebook and stood up, giving both women a quizzical look.

'I do wonder about the coincidence.'

'What on earth are you talking about?' Joyce sounded a little more strident than she had intended.

'Well, you in particular, Joyce, have been in the general area of a few of the cases I've worked on over the last couple of years, and now you're right in the middle of one.'

'I'm nowhere near the middle, I'm on the periphery. I'm so close to the periphery, I'm in danger of falling off.'

Harnby gave the smallest of smiles, but her eyes were practically grinning and Joyce knew she was being teased.

'We'll be here all weekend,' she said haughtily, 'and if we hear anything, we'll be very happy to pass it on.'

'When you say here, I'm guessing you mean *right here*.' Harnby looked over at the bar, the mischievous twinkle making her eyes dance. 'I hope they stocked up.'

'What are you saying?' Joyce asked. Harnby smiled again; this time the grin reached her mouth.

'Enjoy your stay, ladies. I'm sure I'll see you over the next couple of days.'

'What is she insinuating?' Joyce asked as Harnby left the two women and went to rejoin her colleagues. 'That we're a pair of lushes?' Joyce was both put out and surprised. Harnby had made jokes about Joyce's personal habits in the past, but it never failed to astonish her; the DS looked so straight-laced.

'Not me,' corrected Ginger, 'you. I've only crossed paths with her very briefly. She knows you better, and she's a detective, which means in all likelihood she's basing that comment on solid evidence.'

'I like a drink – who doesn't? – and at my age, I deserve a little of what I like.' Joyce knew she sounded defensive, but felt the need to stick up for her reputation.

'A little?' Ginger raised a single eyebrow. Joyce wondered how long she had been practising that. 'Come on, there's no point arguing with facts. Let's find Dennis. I need a room apart from anything, then we'll see if there's something we can do to help.'

Joyce gave a little huff, eyed the champagne bottle that was sitting in ice, and then followed her friend out of the door.

Lush, she thought, *how dare she?* before checking her watch to see how long it was until 5pm, cocktail hour.

6

---

*D*ennis had just finished speaking to a police officer and was moving to the reception desk to check out a couple. At least, Ginger assumed they were a couple; the man was quite a bit older than the woman, but they had the air of being together. She was perfectly turned out, her makeup delicate and beautifully applied; he was handsome and clearly worked hard on maintaining his tan.

In contrast, Dennis looked tired. The glow of energy that Ginger was used to seeing emanate from him at all times had gone, but he still managed a warm smile and friendly goodbye as he saw the guests off, the man giving him a firm handshake before they went. Dennis's pocket handkerchief had slipped down out of sight and he'd clearly been running his fingers through his hair more than a couple of times. He had always been very proud of his full head of hair, and Ginger was used to him stopping to check it in mirrors and windows at every available opportunity, but right now it looked less than perfect.

'Is everything okay' Ginger asked, knowing it was actually a pretty stupid question.

'I suppose so. I'm just grateful we have only a small number of guests. None of their rooms will be affected as they are all on either the ground or the first floor. I have no idea how long the police will want the top floor closed off. I'm just hoping we can reopen in time to honour all the bookings I have lined up for it next week.'

'When are people due to start staying in those rooms?'

'Friday. We have a drinks party planned, thought we'd make it an event and combine the opening of the top floor with the launch of Tim's exhibition.' Tim was Dennis's boyfriend and The Lodge was hosting an exhibition of his work in the bar, although a number of his paintings were already in permanent positions around the hotel. Dennis moved his hand away from the mouse and leant on the desk, letting out a long sigh. 'I know it's just a lick of paint and some new furniture here and there, but it was an added excuse to open the bubbly.'

Ginger could sense Joyce's ears pricking up at the sound of the word 'bubbly'.

'What can we do?' she asked. 'There must be some way we can help.'

'There's honestly nothing. We just have to put up with the hotel looking like an episode of *CSI* and wait for the guests to start returning throughout the day. It will be easy enough to continue with a level of normality for them; they never went to the top floor anyway.'

'And how about you?' Ginger turned to the woman who had been standing silently next to Dennis the whole time. Her smart navy skirt suit had the logo of the hotel sewn into the fabric. A cream silk shirt and shiny navy court shoes finished off the look. Her dark brown bobbed hair was similar to Harnby's, but was softer and less like a helmet. If anything, she seemed a little bewildered.

'Me? Oh, I'm okay. I just can't believe that Caroline is gone. None of us can.'

Dennis seemed to perk up a little as he remembered his

manners. 'Barbara, these are my friends, Joyce and Ginger. They're staying at the hotel. Ladies, this is Barbara Dwyer, the best receptionist in the Peak District.'

Barbara smiled. 'Nice to meet you both.'

'You knew Caroline well?' Ginger asked.

'Reasonably. We weren't friends, but we would chat whenever she came in to work. Everyone got on with her, I think. I can't imagine anyone wanting to kill her.'

'You *think* everyone got on with her?' Joyce stepped forward and leaned over Ginger's shoulder, a strong whiff of Chanel No. 5 following her. Barbara glanced between Ginger and Joyce.

'I think so. I never saw anyone argue with her, and there isn't much in the way of gossip or people falling out here at The Lodge. We enjoy being here, Dennis makes it fun.' She looked at her boss, who gave her arm a gentle squeeze.

'Were you here on the desk all morning?' Joyce had moved even closer and Ginger was starting to feel a bit crowded.

'Most of it. I had to pop in to the office a couple of times.'

'Did you see anyone unusual come in and go upstairs?'

Ginger decided it was time to intervene. 'What are you doing, Joyce?' she demanded. 'I'm sure poor Barbara has already been quizzed by the police.'

'Just curious. No harm in that, is there?... So, did you see anyone?'

'Joyce, let it go. They've all had a shock.'

'It's fine, I don't mind,' said Barbara. 'A number of workmen were going up and down.'

'I know it's a Saturday, but it's the final push to get everything finished,' Dennis explained.

'I recognised most of them because they've been here the last couple of months,' Barbara continued. 'But I couldn't be certain I knew every single one of them, and someone could have slipped past.'

'So it would have been easy enough for someone to head

upstairs unnoticed and murder Caroline before coming down the same way and no one raising an eyebrow?'

Barbara looked at Dennis with an expression of horror.

'Dear God, woman! Come with me.' Ginger grabbed Joyce's arm, spun her round and, with a hand placed firmly on her back, steered her into the bar. 'What the hell are you playing at? They've just lost their colleague and, I'm sure on some level, friend. Added to which, she was murdered here, in this hotel, just above our heads. Go easy on them.'

'I understand all that, I'm not a complete ogre.'

Ginger made sure her face expressed how she felt about that.

'Wipe that look off your face! Now, listen to me. You heard Dennis, they want to open up the top floor with a small shindig on Friday. Toast the new wallpaper. The murder is going to hang over them for as long as it takes to solve it. The police will be coming and going, staff will be interviewed and re-interviewed. It's going to appear in the papers, which may or may not be good for business, and either way, it'll prevent them from moving on. They need this to be solved, to have the killer identified, to have their friend or colleague or Mary, Queen of Scots or whoever laid to rest so their lives can go on. Agreed?'

'Agreed. I sense you're heading somewhere with this.'

'Of course I am. I don't ramble pointlessly, I never have. I don't ramble at all, come to think of it.'

'Sure about that?'

'Stop it, you're distracting me. My point is that if we can figure out who killed Caroline, and quickly, then Dennis and everyone else here can move on.'

'I have heard of an organisation called the police. I believe they're quite good at this, and I seem to recall they were here. Some of them still are.' As if overhearing the conversation, a uniformed officer stuck his head into the bar, apologised for interrupting and left. 'See?'

'How good they are could be up for debate. We're here, on

site. You know Dennis very well and I'm sure you could get any information we need from him. While we're staying here, we'll have plenty of time to get to know the staff and needle anything important out of them, and if all goes to plan, we can identify the killer and Friday night will be a real celebration.'

'I'm not sure *celebration* is the right word to use,' was the reply, but Ginger couldn't help feeling that Joyce had a point. Over the years, she and Dennis had stuck together. They'd kept each other's confidences since they were thirteen years old. They had bailed each other out of a variety of legal and illegal scenarios. It would be nice to solve this, to fix a problem for her friend and help him through what was going to be a dreadful week. Ginger didn't even know if the full enormity of what had happened had hit him yet. He was probably just trying to keep the team going and answer all the questions that were being fired at him.

Ginger looked at Joyce. Her friend's eyes were wide and clear, the certainty that her plan was the right thing to do stamped firmly on her face. Weirdly, she was also standing stock-still and Ginger was tempted to poke her to see if she hadn't turned to ice.

'Okay, I'm in.'

'Marvellous.' Joyce's features softened into a broad grin. 'I knew you'd see sense. Now then, we need a magnifying glass and a deerstalker hat.'

'We need *what?*'

'I'm joking. Go and get Dennis. What we really need is to make a start.'

7

*G*inger had decided that it would be a nice idea to get Dennis out of the hotel for a while, give him a change of scenery and some fresh air. This had required Joyce to make a shoe change as Ginger had also concluded that it meant going for a walk. Not that this was a problem as Joyce never went anywhere without multiple pairs of shoes that would cover all eventualities. Although Joyce could never be considered much of a walker (the word 'hike' made her shiver), she had brought with her a pair of black knee-high boots which would go perfectly well with her current outfit. They would do the job.

The hotel sat on the edge of the Pavilion Gardens, a restored Victorian pleasure garden which was very used to people perambulating through its landscaped grounds, although not necessarily for the purpose of discussing murder. All the trio had to do was cross the road and they were walking around a small man-made lake, past cascades, and over footbridges that spanned the narrow River Wye. The gardens were not yet bursting with an array of greens, let alone colourful flowers as it was too early in the year, so there was a drabness to the scene which fitted their conversation well, and the air around them felt damp. The bandstand stood empty, anticipating the spring and a chance to entertain. The tracks of the miniature railway were waiting for the next train of the day to trundle past carrying a handful of uncertain-looking children, all bundled up against the cold day. Joyce glanced across at the Opera House at the far end of the Pavilion, the twin-domed towers framing its ornate glass canopy. Its stately position as an Edwardian architectural jewel was diminished by the gloom of the grey skies overhead.

Dennis had arranged for takeout coffees from the hotel kitchen, which Joyce was very grateful for. She had a feeling it was going to be a long day and they still hadn't had lunch. The three of them sipped their coffees now as they walked slowly side by side down the wide paths.

'Have you heard from Tim?' Ginger asked.

'Regularly since I told him about Caroline, he's been making sure I'm okay. He's gone to an art exhibition in Sheffield; he was desperate to see Anish Kapoor's work, but he's already on his way back.'

'Tell us about Caroline,' Joyce instructed him. If she was honest, her little speech back at the hotel had been more a show of bravado than anything, she'd got caught up in the moment. But as the minutes had ticked by, the idea had started to settle into her mind and the questions were shooting around her brain. 'I want to know everything about her.'

'I'm not sure I can tell you everything. But I'll tell you what I can.' Bundled in a long black coat, Dennis could have easily been mistaken for a spy, passing on information gathered in shady undercover actions. But the softness in his face and voice would soon put paid to that image. 'She came to work for me two years ago. She was raised here in Buxton, but left the area when she went to university. Her mother still had a house in the town and when she died, Caroline inherited it and decided to come back. As she told it to me, she didn't have any ties anywhere else, remained fond of Buxton and took it as a sign that she should come here and try to build a life for herself.

'She was looking for work and we were one of the places she sent her CV to. She'd done customer service work in the past, but the only job I had available was as a cleaner in the housekeeping team and she took it.'

'How old was she?'

'About forty-two-ish. I can't remember.'

'Was she meant to be at work today?' Ginger asked.

'No, she's only part time and she wasn't down to work.'

'And the tour guiding?'

'She loved history and went on a couple of local guided tours – the ones where the guide is dressed in historical costume – and it inspired her. She was particularly interested in Mary, Queen of Scots, did a lot of research, and then offered to give tours to guests. But she could talk to them about general Buxton history too so it was a great bonus to have her on staff.

'There are a couple of guides who do this in Buxton, but in the summer months there are enough tourists to give them all work. If I got a special request from a guest and Caroline was at work, then I could swap a few things round on the staff rota and free her up to give a tour. She was my on-call Queen Mary, so to speak.'

'Was she any good?' Joyce wasn't sure about the idea of trailing behind someone in costume out in public. She'd feel rather silly.

'Excellent. I got nothing but positive feedback and I'm sure she was making a fair bit of extra money in tips, especially from the American guests.'

The trio stopped on a metal-framed footbridge and Joyce looked over at the ducks. The idea of duck down was appealing; she was getting cold.

'What about the other guides, was there any competition? Any feuds with threats of duels at dawn?'

'None. If you're looking for people who might have reason to kill her, I can't think of anyone. She was a quiet, conscientious worker. I don't recall her being particularly close with anyone and I don't believe she was dating anyone. When she wasn't guiding, she pretty much faded into the background.'

Ginger looped her arm into his. 'But someone wanted her dead, Dennis, and they'd been thinking about it for a while.'

'What makes you say that?'

'There was no sign of a struggle, for a start. The room was spotless, if you exclude the corpse. Also, you've just told us she wasn't scheduled to work, so presumably she was meeting someone. Unless a guest had asked her to do a tour.'

'No, not that I'm aware of.'

'So why was she at the hotel, unless someone had asked to meet her? And as there was no sign of a struggle, they knew what they wanted to do and they could do it without her having time to call out or struggle enough to make a mess of the room.'

She's good, thought Joyce. Dennis's expression turned from one of curiosity to concern. There were a few moments of silence as everyone let that idea settle into their minds before Joyce spoke.

'There is one thing puzzling me, Dennis. You haven't asked why Ginger and I are so interested in all of this.'

'I don't need to. If Ginger has a reason, then I trust her. Besides which, we've known each other for over fifty years. We tell each other everything.'

'I want to hear more about how the two of you met, but I'd rather we did it indoors, if you don't mind. Can we...?'

Ginger looped her other arm though Joyce's and spun her and Dennis round to face the other way, pulling them in the direction of the hotel.

8

'Ed, will you carry these ladies' bags down to the Stanage Suite?' Dennis had just finished finding Ginger and Joyce accommodation on the ground floor and called over a member of staff. 'It's two en-suite rooms with a shared living room, so you girls can make yourself properly at home.'

'So long as the bedrooms are far enough away that I don't have to listen to her snore.'

Ginger was confused. How would Joyce know about her sleeping habits?

'You've never heard me snore.' Ginger did snore, but she wasn't going to admit that to Joyce. 'We've never slept in the same room.'

'No, but you look like a snorer.'

Ginger briefly glanced in Dennis's direction. The corner of his mouth was trying to wiggle its way into a smile, but he was winning the battle. He knew very well that she snored.

'Ladies, if you'll follow me.' A lanky youth picked up their bags and led the way.

He'll be quite good-looking in a few years, mused Ginger. *Right now, he's all arms, legs and big feet.*

'Is there anything else I can help you with?' The youth set their luggage down in the hallway leading into the suite and paused before leaving the room. Ginger wondered whether she was meant to tip him before remembering she didn't have any change on her so he was out of luck.

Joyce came to the rescue with a five pound note. 'Yes, there is. Do you have a minute?'

'Errr, yes.' He looked at the striking woman with her well-applied makeup (Ginger hesitated to use the phrase 'war paint' in case it turned out that Joyce could read minds) and bright pink outfit. He appeared too nervous to say no.

'Have you worked here long?'

'Two years. I'm part time, I'm at college the rest of the week.'

'You must have known Caroline well. I'm so sorry, today's events will have been a dreadful shock to you all.'

'Yeah, kind of, I s'pose. I mean, how does someone get murdered here? It's kind of crazy.'

'Crazy indeed. So, were you friends?'

The young man laughed, and then reined himself in. 'Me and Caroline? God, no. I mean, she was a lot older than me, it would have been like hanging out with me mum.'

'But you talked to her?'

'Oh yeah, she was alright to pass the time of day with, and she'd always help you out.'

Ginger stayed back; she was enjoying watching Joyce try to talk to a teenager who probably thought they were both approaching 100 years of age.

'Did she get on with everyone?'

'I guess so.'

'Do all the team get on with each other?'

Ed paused. 'Err, yeah, I s'pose.'

'It must have been hard, when the thefts were happening. Weren't you all wondering who it was, if it was someone you were working with?'

That apparently took Ed by surprise and he didn't seem to know how to respond. Ginger stepped forward, starting to feel sorry for him.

'Thanks, Ed. We don't need anything else, you've been very helpful.' He left the room as quickly as he could. 'Poor lad. I think we terrified him.'

Joyce laughed at Ginger's concern. 'Good to keep people on their toes.'

'You're evil.'

'Yes and it has served me well. Now then, let's see this room.'

The Stanage Suite, like the other rooms on the ground floor, was named after a location in the area, in this case Stanage Edge, a gritstone escarpment about forty minutes' drive away and popular with rock climbers. It was much brighter than the Queen Mary room, pale grey walls forming the backdrop to an array of antique furniture which had all been updated in bold colours. A purple sofa had a red armchair at one end and a blue one at the other, all with gold wooden edging. An enormous painting of Stanage Edge dominated one wall, the wild and blustery weather shown spectacularly well in the sweeping brushstrokes. Tartan curtains made of the same shades of purple, blue and red as the furniture framed the windows, the lack of a view concealed with net curtains. The large light fitting was made from two dozen bell jars, while a taxidermied squirrel watched them from a shelf in the corner. Ginger promptly stuck it in a cupboard.

'I'm not having that bloody thing eyeballing me all the time. Gives me the creeps. I've told Dennis to get rid of them, but they're all over the place and he's given them all names.'

'This is more like it,' declared Joyce, picking up a cushion to examine the picture of the stag on it in more detail. 'I've no idea what you'd call this style, but it's certainly more cheerful than that room upstairs.' She peered through both bedroom doors. 'And no dead body on either bed. I'm having this one, unless you have any objections?'

Ginger didn't; she was just grateful that Joyce had both agreed to come and was now happy to stick around. She'd have volunteered to sleep on the sofa if that had been required, but she simply smiled and nodded.

'I'm going to freshen up,' said Joyce, 'I'll meet you in the bar. It's almost cocktail hour and I plan on devouring most of the bar menu to make up for the lack of lunch, and… I want to spend more time with Dennis. I'm sure he can tell me all sorts of scandalous gossip about you.'

Ginger made her way to her own room, rather nervous about how loose Dennis's tongue could get after a couple of martinis.

9

*J*oyce knew a thing or two about design, and was impressed by how much care and attention Dennis had taken in creating a fun hotel which had something for everyone, no matter what their taste. She hadn't paid too much attention to the bar the last time she was in here – hardly surprising having just found a dead body – so she made up for it now with a thorough scrutiny.

It was a grand room, cream walls offset by steel blue inlays with a delicate pattern just visible within the paint. A dark blue carpet added depth and made the cream leather sofas and armchairs stand out. Low glass-topped tables with gold legs gave a faintly Art Deco feel. A shiny black piano stood in the far corner.

On the walls was a collection of artwork by the same person. Tim, she assumed. The pictures were mixed media: watercolours, photographs, newspaper cuttings all combining to capture the beauty and history of Buxton. One showed the elegant Georgian Crescent, a beautiful painting of it overlaid with a black-and-white photograph of guests arriving in the 1930s. Just visible through the paint were the words of newspaper clippings.

Another showed Solomon's Temple, a Victorian folly which overlooked the town. The temple itself was more like a sketch, the backdrop of greens and blues a mixture of paint and shreds of paper.

Joyce wasn't entirely sure what you would call the overall look of the room, but it was certainly stylish and calming, and had more than a touch of glamour. Perfect for those who found some of the more quirky choices elsewhere in the hotel a bit too 'out there'.

Dennis was behind the bar and had clearly spotted her admiring the room.

'We finished this a month ago; I'm rather proud of it.'

Joyce nodded approvingly. The bar stools were equally glamorous: white leather seats and a rail for feet which could have been designed with her exact height in mind. She gracefully stepped up and into the curve of the seat and crossed one leg over the other. Joyce wasn't what anyone would call skinny, but she verged on slim and had curves in all the right places, coupled with a tendency to wear clothing tight enough to show off those curves in their full glory. Even Dennis, she noted, couldn't help but watch as she arranged herself to ensure her best assets were on display.

After all, she thought, *you never know who might walk in. It might even be husband number four.*

Joyce had chosen an elegant black dress with a neckline that plunged low enough to need an oxygen tank and flippers. Large gold hoop earrings dangled from her lobes, while a necklace made of hundreds of hoops of varying sizes covered most of her décolletage. A matching bracelet hanging from each wrist looked a little like elegant shackles that she had only partially broken free of.

Dennis now looked a little calmer, certainly less flustered than before. On the surface at least, he had recovered quickly from the shock of the day's events. He certainly seemed as though the bar was his natural habitat, a place where he would feel most at ease and able to forget that earlier the same day, a body had been found in his own hotel. Joyce took this as a sign that he would be able to make her a superb cocktail; besides which, he was bound to want to impress the travelling companion of his best friend.

She ran her eyes across the bottles on the long glass shelves behind the bar, tapping a fingernail on the counter as she took in the selection. If truth be told, she wanted Dennis to spot the polish: half jet black, half gold with a vibrant sparkle. Gins appeared to be a speciality here at The Lodge bar, but there was also a bourbon collection that she knew would satisfy Ginger's tastes.

After giving her a few minutes, Dennis spoke.

'May I suggest a glass of Moët to begin? Once Ginger arrives, I can make you some cocktails I designed personally, but for now, you might prefer to relax with something a little more familiar.'

'That sounds like a marvellous suggestion, Dennis.' Her plummy speech had returned. Ginger always teased her about that, but Joyce felt that she was simply adapting to her surroundings, a verbal chameleon, if you will. She also knew she was as good as any lord or lady she had met and wasn't going to have any of them look down on her. It was her firmly held opinion that she really did belong in the finer surroundings and in a past life had been a duchess, or maybe a king's mistress.

'Which of the Egyptian pyramids did you raid to get all that?' Ginger pulled herself up onto the stool next to Joyce, never once taking her eyes off the gold that twinkled in the bar lights. 'Is it real?'

'You'll never get close enough to find out,' replied Joyce as she stretched out a hand for the champagne Dennis had finished pouring.

'Oh, I don't know, we are sharing a suite. I can give it the once-over before placing a pillow over…'

'Ginger, darling,' interrupted Dennis, 'put the claws away. What would you like to drink, or can I assume you would like your usual?'

'She knows she's my new favourite person.' Ginger winked at Joyce, who raised her glass at her.

'I'm offended.' Dennis placed a hand dramatically over his heart.

'I said *new*; you're my *old* favourite and always will be. Yes please, my usual, no one makes them quite like you.'

'One Old Fashioned coming up.'

'I assume you're joining us?' Ginger asked.

'After a day like today? I'm going to spend as much of the evening as possible on that side of the bar, only popping back here to refill our glasses. Lisa, my bar manager, will be here shortly.' After giving the drink a final stir and garnishing it with orange peel, he passed it to Ginger. 'Here you are, my darling. It rather matches your outfit.' Ginger had chosen an amber coloured silk t-shirt and loose fitting black silk trousers. Simple yet, Joyce had to admit, very elegant.

Joyce and Ginger perused a menu while Dennis quickly whipped up a cocktail for himself. Once he was done, Ginger raised her glass.

'To Caroline.'

'Yes, to Caroline,' Dennis seconded. They all took a long drink.

'Better than mine?' Ginger asked, nodding towards Dennis's martini glass.

'No offence, my sweet, but the two cannot be considered in the same sentence.'

'How do you like them?' Joyce enquired. She hadn't been paying attention as he'd mixed it.

'Ah, this is a dirty martini.' He took another sip. 'Fabulous! It tastes like a truck stop, as our American brethren would say.'

Joyce imagined the British equivalent: a service station on the

M1, which conjured up visions of a dirty lorry and an overweight oil-stained driver who lit a fag as soon as he clambered down from his cab. She'd happily give the drink a pass.

'Go on, try it.' Dennis slid his glass along the bar towards Joyce, who tried not to look visibly appalled. He stared at her, an encouraging smile on his lips. Ginger was watching too. Reluctantly, Joyce slowly picked up the glass and took a tiny sip, then screwed up her face as she forced herself to swallow. The salty olivey flavour did nothing for her.

Ginger roared with laughter. 'I'm afraid you've not got yourself a convert there, Dennis. Can't say I blame you, Joyce, bloody awful things.'

Joyce took a large swig of champagne to cleanse her palate, and then changed the subject.

'So, you two dated in school?'

'We were love's young dream from the age of thirteen until, hmmm, sixteen? Weren't we, my darling?' Dennis kissed the back of Ginger's hand.

'Yes, but we weren't meant to be.'

'No, it was very sad, but she didn't have hairy legs or a beard. Which turned out to be essential requirements of mine.'

'I'm not sure you could say that about me now.'

Joyce laughed as Ginger stroked her chin and plucked at a wiry white hair.

'Well, there you are,' Joyce offered. 'Maybe you could give it another go.'

'Unless something else has appeared over time, I'm not hopeful. Besides which, I think my chap might have something to say about it.' Dennis checked his watch. 'And he'll be here in the next hour so our window of opportunity is decidedly narrow. No, I think that we must accept that the gods were not on our side. But we do have the most beautiful of friendships.'

'And I have a plus one whenever I need one,' Ginger added.

'I do feel a little usurped in that department.' Dennis looked at

Joyce with a comic expression of haughty jealousy. 'Although, if I'm going to be usurped at all, I can't imagine a more delightful and wildly stylish creature to be usurped by.'

Joyce blushed beneath her makeup, pleased that not a patch of bare skin was exposed. She was only human and enjoyed a compliment as much as the next person.

'So, any juicy gossip?' she asked. 'Anything I can use as leverage in future disagreements?'

Dennis pretended to be deep in thought. 'Well, there was the time she let down the tyres on the head teacher's car. And she poisoned a teacher, and led the girls in a strike when they weren't allowed to play football. She also betrayed me with Richard Strange.'

'He *was* strange too,' Ginger confirmed.

'So why did you choose him to betray Dennis with?'

'Because Dennis was paying far too much attention to David Essex and I was trying to get him to notice me, and poor Richard just happened to be the first lad to ask me out.'

'If we'd been a little older, we might have spotted my interest in David Essex as a sign.'

'What of, your bad taste in music?' Joyce asked.

'My preference for gentlemen.'

'I want to hear more about you poisoning a teacher.' Joyce looked at her friend with glee.

'I didn't really poison him, it was only laxatives. I was ultimately a good girl.'

'Ginger Salt, a good girl? We all know that's a questionable assertion.' A tall, slim man with a neat beard and piercing blue eyes had walked into the bar and wrapped Ginger in a hug from behind. His denim shirt was wrinkled, but still looked smart beneath a black leather jacket. 'It's good to see you, my dear. I believe you've had quite the day. And you must be Joyce Brockle-hurst, very pleased to make your acquaintance. I'm just sorry that it's after such a tragic event.' He shook Joyce's hand while she noted how perfect the line of his beard was.

'Joyce, meet my boyfriend, Tim Starling.'

Tim walked behind the bar and gave Dennis a kiss. 'How are you?' he asked with genuine concern.

'Bearing up. Better now I've had one of these.' Dennis held his half-empty glass in the air. 'How was it with the police?'

'Straightforward. I had my tickets for the train and the exhibition, so they asked me a couple of questions and that was it.' He looked at the two women and registered the confusion on their faces. 'I had to go and give a statement to the police to explain where I was this morning. I don't mind, I know it's only routine.'

'And while you were being interrogated, I've had the most delightful company for distraction,' declared Dennis, lightening the mood. 'Now why don't we move to a table? Lisa can take care of things here.' Dennis mouthed a thank you at a young woman who had just walked into the bar. Very tidily dressed in a black skirt and white shirt, a neat ponytail hanging down her back, she smiled at her boss warmly, and then immediately turned to serve a customer.

As they walked towards a table in the far corner, Joyce turned to Dennis.

'I'm surprised this place isn't heaving. You'd think you'd become the hot spot for the night: *come get a drink in the hotel where Mary, Queen of Scots was murdered.*'

They all sank simultaneously into marshmallow-like leather armchairs.

'We've made it residents only for tonight for precisely that reason,' explained Dennis. 'I don't want this place to become a freak show.'

Joyce looked around the bar, feeling grateful. The idea of such a nice space being overrun with weirdos made her shiver.

'Is there anything more you can tell us about Caroline?' she asked. Both she and Ginger had made themselves comfortable, and now looked as if they were conducting an interview as Dennis and Tim settled down opposite.

'She was part of our hotel family, she'd been with us since she moved back to Buxton a couple of years ago. I have no idea who'd want to kill her.'

'I do.' As they all swung round to face her, Joyce realised she might have made a little too blunt a statement.

inger stared at her friend, more than a little surprised. It seemed like they'd only been in the place five minutes; she knew Joyce could be quite observant, but this was a record.

'What are you talking about? How can you know?'

'Okay, so I don't know for sure, but I do have an idea. Dennis, you said you'd had some thefts in the hotel, items being stolen from guests' rooms.'

'Yes, it's been happening on and off for a couple of months now. Phones, watches, iPads, that sort of thing. Nothing for the last two weeks, though.'

'What if Caroline had found out who was stealing from the guests? Not only would they get in a lot of trouble and, I assume, lose their job, but they would have to face the police and lose an extra source of income. I admit that murder is rather an extreme response to cover up the theft of a few phones and watches, but it's not entirely beyond belief.'

It was a rather extreme conclusion too, but Ginger had to acknowledge that it was a good place to start. Dennis and Tim glanced at each other.

'You have a point,' Dennis said.

'Have you told the police about the thefts?'

'In some cases, it depended on what the guest wanted to do, but I told the detective sergeant all about it when she interviewed me.' Dennis stared into his drink. 'Do you think if we'd done more, we could have prevented Caroline's murder?'

Ginger reached across and took hold of his hand. 'You can't think that way; you are in no way responsible for what happened.' She wanted to distract him. 'Where was everyone around the time that she was killed?'

'It's hard to be precise. I know who was on duty and where they were meant to be, but the staff can get pulled away to other jobs or to assist guests. Barb was able to identify the workmen on site: it was Graham Bennett's lads. She says Graham was here briefly too.'

'Graham Bennett is?' Joyce asked.

'The latest in a long line of Bennett's Family Carpenters. He's a good man and bloody good at what he does, he's the only carpenter I'll allow on site. Mind you, business has really taken off for him and he's going to be harder to get hold of in the future. He's increasingly working on older buildings of historical significance.

'Other than that, there are the guests staying on the ground floor who come and go. But it's a hotel: it would be easy for someone to come in off the street and we can't be 100% sure they'd get spotted. Certainly anyone can come in to go to the bar or eat in the restaurant, but neither of those had opened by the time you arrived here, so that's unlikely. Between Barb and the staff I've spoken to, no one saw anything or anyone out of place.'

'What about fire exits?' asked Joyce. 'Are they alarmed?'

'No, not all of them.'

'So her killer could have come in that way?'

'They would have had to come in through the main entrance

first and prop the door open, or have someone inside do it for them.'

'Cameras?'

'In key areas, yes, and there was no one suspicious on them.'

'Which tells us the killer either knew the hotel well enough to bypass them, or was someone who you would expect to see on camera.'

Ginger's final remark left them all silent for a minute or two.

'What about friends or other family? Someone who might be able to tell us if there was anyone she had fallen out with?'

Ginger was grateful for Joyce's question changing the direction of the conversation. Dennis answered.

'I don't know much about her private life, but I know she had someone she would study with. They'd travel to Manchester together to go to the libraries there. Madeleine. She'd occasionally meet Caroline from work and she came to a couple of the events we held. Nice enough. She might be able to tell you more.'

'Any idea how we can track her down?'

Dennis looked at Ginger. 'What are you up to, Ms Salt? There's a look you get in your eyes when you're up to something and I can see it now. I'm never sure whether to be excited or terrified.'

'Have I ever done anything that either of us has regretted?'

Joyce laughed at the face that Dennis pulled. 'How long have you got? Almost every hangover I've ever had is a result of your influence.'

'True, but we always had a lot of fun getting them.'

'Okay, I'll give you that. How about the time I had to have a wooden stake pulled out of my calf?'

'That's because you didn't spend enough time as a child climbing trees. If you had then climbing that fence wouldn't have been a problem.'

'I was thirty-five! We shouldn't have been climbing fences.'

'You have such a limited sense of adventure.'

'Maybe, but I do have a rather cool scar that looks like a flash of lightning on the back of my leg.'

Tim watched the two of them with a comfortable smile; he'd witnessed this sort of banter on a regular basis. Ginger could see from Joyce's expression that her friend was wondering why they were climbing fences in their thirties and probably adding it to her list of questions. One way or another, this was turning out to be a *very* interesting weekend.

11

'So, what do you think?' Joyce had kicked off her shoes and was lying on the sofa in the sitting room adjoining their bedrooms. 'Do you think that we can work this out by Friday?' With all the gold hanging off her against the background of the purple sofa, she thought she resembled an Egyptian queen awaiting the attentions of a servant.

'Definitely,' Ginger replied without hesitation.

'You sound very certain.' Joyce watched with fascination as Ginger did what could only be described as 'slathering' her face with cream.

'We'll have daily access to the staff if we stay here. Dennis will tell us everything he knows, and we already have a plan to visit Madeleine. She's bound to have something useful she can tell us.' Ginger paused with a face that was going to give Joyce night-mares as soon as she fell asleep, her cream-covered fingers hovering in the air. 'Do you really think this is about the thefts?'

'I've no idea, but I wanted to see how Dennis would react and if it would lead to any more information coming your way. Clearly it didn't, but it was worth trying. What the hell is that stuff anyway, cement?'

'Simple, plain cold cream. It was good enough for my mother, it's good enough for me. I don't need any of your overpriced stuff. I bet you have half a dozen different things you layer on before you go to bed.'

Three actually, but Joyce wasn't going to reveal that. She hadn't used cold cream since she was a teenager.

'Cold cream, soap, water. Don't need anything fancier than that and my skin is fabulous, daaaaarling.'

Joyce remained silent. It was obvious that Ginger didn't go to a lot of trouble, and yet she had the smoothest, clearest skin Joyce had ever laid eyes on. She was more jealous than she was ever going to admit.

She decided to change the subject. 'So, our plan of action for tomorrow is...?'

'We find this Madeleine woman, and I'd also like to see where Caroline lived. You can learn a lot about a person from their home. I think we need to find out a bit more about that tour guiding malarkey; I'm wondering if it's a competitive business.'

Joyce thought about the tour guides that worked up at Charleton House. She could think of one whose neck she would merrily wring on a regular basis, but it wasn't a line of work that she associated with homicidal tendencies. But they might find out more about Caroline in general from some of the other guides, so it didn't sound like a complete waste of time.

'Fine by me. Now I do have a couple of questions for you.'

'Okay.' Ginger didn't sound entirely sure about what might be coming next.

'Why would you try and poison a teacher, and why were you climbing fences in your thirties?'

'I've already said, it was laxatives, not poison,' Ginger clarified with obvious relief. 'And that fence? We were running away from the police.'

Ginger walked back through to her room, leaving Joyce hanging. Well, it would only take a couple of drinks to find out more, and find out she would.

12

The following morning, Ginger had gone for a quick romp around the Pavilion Gardens, while Joyce had started her day with a hot soak in the tub, which she felt was entirely reasonable on a Sunday morning in a luxury boutique hotel. After eating breakfast in their room, they'd hunted out Dennis. He had handed over Caroline's address without any questions and, after wrapping up warm, they climbed into Ginger's car.

'Vell, good morning, Madam Vilikof,' Ginger said in her best Russian accent, which was dreadful.

'What are you on about?' asked Joyce as she removed her sunglasses.

'You've got a dead raccoon on your head and that coat looks about right for a Russian winter, not Derbyshire as it crawls its way out of a wet March.'

Joyce brushed a piece of lint off the long woollen camel-coloured coat, and undid the wide belt that had been tied in a neat overhand knot and a couple of the large tortoiseshell buttons. Ginger had cranked up the heating; if Joyce started to melt, then so be it. Ginger sometimes wondered if there was a large industrial unit somewhere that held nothing but Joyce's wardrobe. To date, she hadn't seen her friend wear the same outfit twice, and she had something for every occasion. Right now, Joyce looked like a cross between a Russian spy and Jacques Clouseau; Ginger wasn't sure whether to expect a Russian or French accent the next time she spoke. Ginger was relieved she wasn't carrying an umbrella, she didn't want anyone getting poisoned over the course of the week. One dead body was enough.

It was only a five-minute drive, but Joyce had insisted they go in the car. They drove through the town, past its shops, cafés and art galleries, spotting a bookshop that looked like somewhere Harry Potter would visit, before turning in to an estate that some years ago would have been considered new and modern. They pulled up at the end of a close with a thick bank of trees straight ahead, and two carbon-copy brown-brick houses with red-brick detailing on either side of where they had parked.

Caroline's house was to their right. It looked like a large family home, three bedrooms at least. The driveway was empty.

'Dennis said she couldn't afford a car, and didn't need one. It's only a fifteen-minute walk.' Ginger gave Joyce an intense look as she emphasised the word *walk*.

'I wasn't going to hike here in these boots.'

'A fifteen-minute walk through town is not hiking, not in anyone's book.' Ginger looked at Joyce's feet, clad in knee-high leather boots with heels that could be used to aerate a lawn. They finished off the Russian spy look perfectly. Ginger knew full well Joyce could probably climb Snowdon in them, but she chose to say no more on the matter. 'I thought the police would be here.'

'I guess they finished up here last night. There's still tape over the door, though.' Joyce craned her neck and checked out the houses around them. 'I can't see any movement, no one seems to be paying us any attention.'

'Give it a couple of minutes and they will. This place was

probably crawling with police last night, so the curtains will start twitching any minute. We ought to check the place out and get going.'

'Not necessarily.' Joyce smiled. 'Everyone is going to assume that we're just another pair of police detectives, they're not going to ask any questions of plainclothes officers checking out a few final things.'

'There's nothing plain about your outfit.'

'I should hope not. Come on, let's have a sniff around.'

Ginger watched as Joyce spun her legs around and rose out of the seat like someone who had attended the country's finest deportment school. Ginger placed one hand on the seat, the other on the wheel and hauled herself out of the car seat while holding her breath, swearing to herself that she wasn't going to groan in the way she did as she levered herself out of the sofa at home. She looked over her shoulder as they walked down the driveway. Yes, there it was; the first twitching curtain. Ginger pulled a small notebook out of her pocket and pretended to be reading.

'What have you got there?'

'This is my police notebook and I am reviewing my notes, or at least that's what I want people to think. Go round the back and have a look; I'll stay at the front and look like I have a clear sense of purpose.'

She furrowed her brow and flipped over a page. Joyce strode off round the side of the house, her heels announcing her presence to everyone on the estate, while Ginger gradually made her way to the front window and peered in. The room was dark, the furnishings not doing anything to help. A coffee-coloured sofa and two matching armchairs dominated the room. A dark-brown sideboard sat along one wall, two matching bookcases on opposite sides. The TV wasn't particularly modern. It looked distinctly as though Caroline hadn't made any changes since her mother had died; she'd just moved in and left it as it was. But then if what

Dennis had said was right, she hadn't had a lot of spare cash. The house was paid for, but there wasn't much else.

'Hello?' Ginger spun round, dropping her notepad in the process. 'Sorry, I didn't mean to startle you.' A young woman stood in the middle of the driveway with a carrier bag in each hand. 'Are you the police?'

'Umm, well...' Ginger regained her composure while trying to decide what to say. 'We're looking into the death of Caroline Clatworthy.' That should do it; she hadn't said they were the police, so they couldn't be charged with impersonating officers. She knew they had to avoid that.

'Oh good, I thought I might find someone here. I wondered if I should go to the police station, but I was passing by and thought I'd stop on the off chance.' The woman sounded nervous; Ginger decided it was best to help her out.

'Can I help in any way?'

'Yes, I have these. They're Caroline's.' She looked at the two bags she was holding with an expression of sadness. The longer she looked at the bags, the more defeated she appeared. Ginger was relieved that her pockets were, as usual, stuffed full of tissues; they might come in handy.

'What are they?'

'It's her laptop and research notes. She'd left them at my flat and I thought they might be helpful.'

'Great!' Ginger sounded far too happy about it and toned her voice down. 'That's very helpful and thoughtful, Miss...'

'English, Madeleine English.'

Hurrah, Ginger said – to herself this time. *Now we're getting somewhere.*

13

*J*oyce came round the corner to see Ginger talking to someone who looked like a librarian – a librarian who couldn't afford a decent bag and carried her books around in plastics. As she walked closer, she saw that the young woman was more consciously working towards a 'bookish look'. Her glasses were actually quite trendy; the knitted sweater had a thick cable pattern and looked expensive, and the long green corduroy coat was definitely all the rage amongst certain members of the younger generation. Joyce realised she had been a little harsh, as the woman also looked as though she was barely holding it together.

'Joyce, this is Madeleine English, Caroline's study partner and friend.'

'Nice to meet you.' Joyce offered her hand to Madeleine, but the carrier bags prevented the gesture going any further.

'Madeleine wanted to drop off some of Caroline's things, thought they might be helpful to the police... our investigation.'

'Excellent, thank you. Very thoughtful, very helpful. We can make sure they get into the right hands.'

'So, you don't need them?' Madeleine looked confused, so Joyce kept talking.

'Well, yes, of course, but our colleagues... well, other people will also need...'

This was getting complicated. Joyce hoped that Ginger hadn't given the woman the impression they were indeed the police; the last thing they needed was to be done for impersonating police officers.

'I've finished here,' Joyce was looking at Ginger now, 'so I think we ought to be getting back to the hotel... office... the hotel office where we need to talk to the manager.'

She needed more practice at this. Ginger was looking bug-eyed at her, which Joyce took as a signal of desperate agreement.

'Do you need a lift anywhere?' she asked the young woman. Why the heck had she said that? Joyce wanted to kick herself; things never went well if she was nice to people.

'Thank you, that would be great. I'm going to the railway station.'

'Righto,' Ginger said with more enthusiasm than any police officer Joyce had come across. 'Excuse the state of the car.'

The fifteen-minute journey to the station gave them enough time to discover that Madeleine and Caroline had known each other for eighteen months; they'd met at a talk being given by the author Tracy Borman on her book *Elizabeth's Women*. Caroline was researching Mary, Queen of Scots for her tours, while Madeleine was in the midst of writing a one-woman play about Queen Elizabeth I. They shared material, went to talks together; they'd even had a weekend in London so they could visit the Tower.

Madeleine played with a tissue Ginger had handed to her as she spoke. 'I wouldn't call us close. Caroline was quite private, very focused on her work. I don't really know much about her, but I'm not surprised that the guests at the hotel wanted to spend time listening to her, I could have listened to her talk for hours.

She had a real way of making you feel like the centre of attention, like you were the only one she was telling the story to, even if you were in a group of thirty.'

'And why did you have her laptop?' Ginger looked at Madeleine in the rear-view mirror as she spoke. Joyce wished she wouldn't; they'd already had one near miss.

'We were having a study day, but she was going into the hotel to give a costumed talk to some guests. She was only going to be a couple of hours, so left her things at mine. She was coming back for dinner later, and then we were going to watch a documentary together.'

'Do you know who she was going to meet? Which guests?' Ginger was staring in the mirror again. Joyce wrapped her fingers around the door handle just in case she needed to brace herself in a hurry.

'No, she only said that she'd received a message that some guests wanted to find out more about Mary, and then go on a walking tour of the centre of Buxton.'

'When did she get the message?'

'I don't know, but she didn't say anything the day before when we were planning for her to come over, so it must have been a last-minute thing. She didn't get many requests for tours at this time of year, it's too cold and wet.'

'And do you know who it was that contacted her?'

'No, no idea.'

'If you don't mind me asking,' Joyce turned round to face Madeleine, slightly hampered by the fact that her hat reached the roof of the car and slowed down the process, 'were you and Caroline a couple?'

Madeleine didn't look at all put out by the question. 'No, just friends.'

'How did you find out she'd died?'

'I got a call from a friend – her cousin works in the hotel kitchen. Gossip travels pretty fast round here.'

Joyce attempted to nod. She understood and had had to talk to her own team about that very thing at work on more than one occasion.

'What can you tell us about her research? Was any of it contentious?'

Madeleine laughed at that. 'Not at all. We're talking about tours for tourists. She had an hour or two to walk them round a part of town and give them a few key bits of information, so she wanted to make sure it was all accurate, and she had some personal interests that she pursued away from the tour research. But I never thought it was anything other than the usual stuff.'

Ginger pulled in to the station car park and turned the engine off.

'What should I do with these?' Madeleine held up one of the plastic bags.

'Just leave them on the back seat,' Ginger instructed her kindly. Madeleine opened the door.

'Thanks for the lift and I hope you catch who did this.' She climbed out of the car and waved as she walked off.

Joyce and Ginger turned round in synchronised swivels and stared at the bags on the backseat. Or more precisely, at a murdered woman's laptop and research. Now what?

14

'I don't know one end of a laptop from the other.' They were still staring at the plastic bags and Ginger wasn't sure where to start.

'You have one, though.'

'Gathering dust. I send emails, but that's about it.' That was partly true: Ginger was a fast learner, she just wasn't all that interested. 'Why don't you look at it?' Joyce had one of those smartphone things so she was much better placed to know what to look for. Ginger still used a clam-like mobile phone that folded up. It couldn't take pictures, only phone people and send text messages, and she didn't want any more than that. She didn't like all the distractions that came with modern phones; she listened to the radio while she sewed and that was the only distraction she welcomed. She was dreading the day that the phone died on her – a day which she felt was worryingly close.

'We could probably get arrested, tampering with police evidence, and I wouldn't know what to look for.' Joyce didn't sound very confident either. Neither of them had reached for the bags; they just looked at them as if they might be about to move or make a noise.

They sat in silence for a few more minutes before Ginger spoke.

'This is ridiculous.' She turned the engine back on and threw the car into gear. It made an awful grinding sound.

'Pick a gear, any gear,' Joyce suggested, wincing.

'We're going back to the hotel, and then we should hand over the computer like the helpful citizens we are. That way no one gets suspicious.'

'And the papers?'

'We keep hold of those for a day or two, see if there's anything interesting. Then we hand them in too.'

'And how do we explain that we have them?' Joyce's head was thrown back as Ginger shot out into traffic, beeping her horn as she went.

'We say we ran into Madeleine outside the hotel; she was looking a bit lost and we got talking to her. She had the laptop and didn't know what to do with it, so we offered to bring it inside. We say something similar in a couple of days about the papers. In fact, we could say that we gave her our phone numbers because she looked so upset and we thought she might want to talk. We're just a couple of friendly old dears wanting to help a young woman who has lost her friend in tragic circumstances.'

'I'm glad you didn't add *sweet* to the old dears. *Old* is bad enough.'

'So you agree?'

'Yes, I agree. Pull up just before we get to The Lodge and I'll stuff the papers in my bag.'

Ginger had hold of the laptop as they walked inside The Lodge, and wasn't sure whether to regard it as good fortune or bad luck when she spotted Detective Sergeant Harnby talking to a uniformed officer at the bottom of the stairs. Ginger turned quickly and double-checked Joyce's bag, making sure there were no papers poking out. It did look rather full, but they'd just have to hope that DS Harnby didn't notice. She still couldn't quite believe what they were doing. At best, it was bloody stupid; at worst, they could be arrested.

'Right, here goes,' Ginger muttered, then raised her voice. 'Detective Sergeant Harnby, thank goodness you're here.'

Harnby turned. Ginger rather liked the young woman; despite the funereal wardrobe and boringly neat haircut, Harnby had an air of energy about her. Ginger pictured her marching across the hills of the Peak District on her days off, a rucksack on her back and a compass in her hand. She probably didn't eat sweets and took her own salads into work for lunch. That reminded Ginger that she had a large bar of chocolate in her room and was now longing for a couple of chunks. Okay, the whole thing.

'Hello, ladies.' Harnby looked over Ginger's shoulder. 'Joyce, you look like you've come in from the cold… war.'

Ginger opted not to look at Joyce's face. Anyway, Harnby was right.

'We were handed this, it's Caroline's.'

Harnby's eyes almost popped out of their sockets at the sight of the laptop in Ginger's hands. 'Where did you get this? We knew she had one, but it wasn't at the house.'

'Madeleine…' Ginger pretended to think '…English, that's it. Madeleine English. We ran into her outside the hotel.'

'Why didn't she come in?'

Ginger was stumped. She was starting to sweat.

'She was on her way to the railway station,' Joyce said. 'She seemed quite upset too. She was very relieved when we offered to bring it in.'

'Did she give you her contact details? We'll need to talk to her.'

Ginger glanced up at Joyce. If they said no, that was the plan for explaining the sudden appearance of Caroline's notes out of the window. They'd worry about that at the time, Ginger decided.

'No, I'm afraid not, but this is a small town and I'd recognise her. If we see her around, we'll get her contact details for you.'

'Don't worry, we'll track her down. Her details are probably on the laptop.' Harnby held Ginger's gaze for a moment. She wasn't entirely convinced by their story, Ginger could tell.

'Well, I'm exhausted. I need a sit down and a cup of tea,' Joyce declared, grabbing Ginger's arm and pulling her down the corridor towards their room before she had a chance to say anything else.

'Exhausted? It's barely lunchtime.'

'It was all I could think of; it was that or we give Harnby time to decide that it's worth interrogating us. Get out while the going's good, I say. I want to see if there's anything useful in these notes. For all we know, the name of the killer is currently stuffed in my bag.'

15

*J*oyce had immediately called for a pot of tea and two large slices of cake to be delivered to their room. She was learning that the cold always made Ginger hungry and thought it better to feed her instead of listening to her complain. While Ginger made her slice disappear with the speed of a magician, Joyce spread the notes out over the large coffee table.

There were a couple of notebooks and a stack of loose-leaf A4 papers that were secured with an elastic band. She still couldn't believe what they had done, striding right past Harnby with evidence in their bag. There was no escaping the fact that it was idiotic, they hadn't been thinking straight, but now they had them, they may as well get on with it. Joyce wasn't looking forward to this; she'd rather be out talking to people, charming them over a glass of wine, wheedling information out of them, but this was what they had to work with right now.

'Where do we start?' asked Ginger through a mouthful of rich, dark chocolate cake.

'No idea. Pick one and get stuck in. I haven't a clue if this is going to be of any use, but I think we give it an hour, then we head to the bar and see who is around. We need to talk to more of the guests and see if they know anything.'

The long ruby-red nail on Joyce's forefinger ran down the page. She'd put on a pair of round tortoiseshell reading glasses and now felt like a sexy super-sleuth. After a few minutes, she threw her legs up on the sofa; all she needed was a cigarette in a long, slim holder and a glass of champagne and she would have been at home in a James Bond film.

'Pass me that green notebook, will you?'

Ginger put down the paper she was reading and handed the notebook over.

'And can you slide my tea closer?'

'What did your last slave die of?'

'It wasn't natural causes.' Joyce peered at her friend over the frames of her glasses and Ginger tutted as she slid the cup over.

An hour later and Joyce was still none the wiser. She'd pulled a particularly soft woollen blanket over her legs, while Ginger was now sitting on the floor with papers scattered around her. Not only was all the cake gone, but between them they'd devoured Ginger's secret stash of chocolate.

'Well, so far I've learnt more about Mary, Queen of Scots than I ever wanted to know, and more about Buxton's spa waters than I ever thought possible.' Ginger sighed before continuing. 'But nothing is standing out at me, and I still haven't touched the other half of the pile. Anything leap out at you?'

'Not a dicky bird. I've read this last page three times; her handwriting isn't the best.' Joyce spun into a sitting position and wiggled her toes in the thick carpet. 'I have an idea. It will save us time and means we can go for lunch with a clear plan of action.'

'And that is?'

'I work with someone who would enjoy going through all this. You've met him: Mark Boxer, one of the tour guides up at

Charleton. Infuriating bugger, but if there's anything to be found in here, he'll find it.'

'Then call him. My back's killing me. I'll even buy him dinner.'

Joyce dug her mobile phone out from the bottom of her bag and placed it on the table. Putting it on speakerphone, she called Mark's number. He picked up after only one ring.

'Good afternoon, Medusa, run out of food for your snakes? Need me to drop off a few mice?'

'If I was going to feed anything to snakes, it would be you. Now, I hate to say this, and I expect you to forget I ever said it out loud...'

'You need my help?'

Joyce closed her eyes. Mark was an irritating know-it-all at the best of times, but over the years, she had grown quite fond of him. He was now *her* irritating know-it-all.

'Yes,' she hissed though her teeth. 'I need your help, or rather, *we* do. I'm here with Ginger. Any chance you could come to Buxton this afternoon? We'd like you to look at some research.'

'Ooh, that sounds intriguing. What is it, are you putting together a study of matricide through the ages? Or perhaps it's your thesis on withering looks and eye rolls of the rich and famous.'

'Just get yourself to The Lodge by the Pavilion Gardens.'

'You moonlighting as a dishwasher in the kitchens? I can picture you in your Marigolds.'

Joyce hung up.

'Idiot. Right, lunch, and it's time to meet some of the other guests.'

$\mathcal{G}$inger had spent many a happy hour in the company of Dennis in some of the country's top restaurants, all in the name of 'research', although the bottom line was they both loved food. A lot. So she knew that Dennis would insist on the finest food, prepared to the highest standards, coming out of The Lodge's kitchen.

They weren't disappointed. Ginger's confit salmon and Joyce's salad of cherry-smoked duck were perfection on a plate, although both secretly admitted that the portions were rather small. As they cleared the last morsels from their plates, Dennis walked over to the table and pulled up a chair.

'Ladies, you seem to have gained the attention of Detective Sergeant Harnby.'

'Really?' That worried Ginger. Had Harnby found out they had kept back Caroline's notes? Dennis laughed.

'She was of the opinion that you might be a bit of a handful and wondered how long you were staying. She sounded quite concerned, for me.'

'And how long *are* we staying?' asked Ginger.

'As long as you like. Well, maybe not quite as long as you like. The rooms you're in are free until the weekend.'

Ginger didn't have anywhere to be, but she knew Joyce had a job to return to at some point, so they really should get on with the task at hand.

'What can you tell us about the guests who were staying when Caroline died?'

Dennis put both elbows on the table, tilting his head in thought.

'Well, there is Mr and Mrs Dalrymple – Marjorie and Marmaduke, if you believe it, although we'd never call him anything other than Mr Dalrymple or sir. Retired, come here on a regular basis. They have family in Buxton and always stay here; they're two doors down from you. You'll recognise them when you see them, they look like a couple of characters out of an Agatha Christie mystery.

'A couple of women were here to escape their kids – left them with their husbands and nearly drank us out of champagne. Left an hour ago.' He looked quickly at Joyce. 'Don't worry, I have a delivery arriving tomorrow. A handful of people I'd never seen before, probably making the most of the reduced prices we offered while the work was being done. A young couple attending a family birthday party. An author researching a book: she's writing a murder mystery set in Buxton, but I think she got more than she bargained for. And finally, there's John Bradbury, local self-made millionaire via the art of plumbing. Likes to stay here whenever there's an event he needs to attend.'

'If he's local, why does he stay over? Couldn't he just get a taxi home?' asked Ginger, looking sidelong at Joyce.

'By local, I mean Derbyshire. He lives about an hour away, which I realise isn't much to most of us, but he doesn't like to bother and he can afford to stay here as often as he likes, so I'm happy to take his money. There is another reason.' Dennis lowered his voice. 'This is where he stays with his mistress.'

Joyce put her knife and fork down. 'In his sixties or there-abouts? Looks like he's spent too much time on a sunbed?'

'That's him. He and his lady friend left yesterday once the police had taken his statement. I imagine he'll be back sometime this week, I can check the bookings. You don't think it could be any of the guests, do you?'

'Why not?' demanded Joyce. 'They had reason to be here, so it's not surprising to see them on CCTV, and Madeleine said that Caroline was coming to talk to a couple of guests who wanted to learn more about Mary, Queen of Scots, so it makes sense that one of them could have arranged to meet her here.'

'Excuse me?' Dennis looked baffled. 'What talk? What guests?'

'We don't know. Madeleine just said it seemed to be a last-minute request, but she had no idea who the guests in question were.'

Dennis's expression turned thoughtful. 'I'm not aware of anyone requesting a talk. Any guest wanting a talk or tour would usually book it through reception. We can see when Caroline is working and give her a call to schedule it. In fact, we're always the middle man.'

'Okay,' said Ginger, 'so whoever killed Caroline requested a talk from her directly – they didn't come through you because that would mean they could be identified – so they knew her well enough to be trusted with her personal phone number. They arranged to meet Caroline on site – in Queen Mary's room, which let's face it is the best place to talk about her – and then killed her.'

'Now then, I haven't seen him before.'

Ginger followed Dennis's eye-line to a tall, slim gentleman who had just entered and was walking their way.

'He definitely looks suspicious.' Joyce raised her voice. 'I'm not sure if he'd kill anyone himself, but I have no doubt people have got very close to wringing his neck.'

'Lovely to see you too, Joyce,' said the newcomer with a wry smile.

'Dennis, meet Mark Boxer. Mark, this is Dennis Matty, general manager of The Lodge.' After Ginger's introduction, the two men shook hands, and then Dennis moved to fetch another chair.

'Thank you. I've been summoned to examine some contraband.'

Joyce got up and went to fetch the 'contraband', leaving Ginger to explain.

'Mark's going to look at some of Caroline's research, see if he can find anything of value in it.'

'Yes, about that.' Mark fixed Ginger with a steady gaze. 'What exactly am I looking at and what am I looking for?' Dennis looked equally intrigued.

'Caroline was doing some research, ostensibly for her tours, into the history of Buxton as a spa town, the links with Mary, Queen of Scots, that sort of thing. We were wondering if there is anything in there that could be considered contentious.'

'That could have got her killed, you mean?'

'Yes, that's right.'

'I'll do my best.'

'That's all we can ask for.' Ginger looked at him kindly; she hoped it would balance out Joyce's scathing comments.

Joyce returned with Caroline's notes in a plastic bag and handed it to Mark.

'Should I be asking where you got these notes from and why they're not with the police?' he asked.

Ginger immediately felt guilty; this could get Mark in trouble too. In the end, it was taking so long for anyone to answer that Mark came to his own conclusions.

'Great. I should have guessed you two would be up to no good.'

'Smart waistcoat,' Joyce commented, changing the subject.

Her tone, although softer than it had been on the phone, still had an edge of reluctance to it, as though it was hard work being nice to Mark. She was right, though; the tweed of his waistcoat had a delicate orange line in the pattern, highlighted by the orange silk back, and Ginger could tell that the tailor was a true craftsman or woman who knew what they were doing. Mark's oiled handlebar moustache had a neat twirl at the end and complemented the look.

Mark pulled out a pocket watch and stood up. 'Well, if that's everything, I should be off. I'll make a start tonight and call you when I'm done. The sooner I get these out of my possession, the better. Anything else, madam?' When Joyce shook her head, he gave a stiff bow towards her, smiled at Ginger, nodded at Dennis, and then started to back out, pretending he was leaving the presence of royalty while narrowly missing a waiter who was carrying a bowl of soup.

'Idiot,' muttered Joyce.

'You need to invite him back as soon as possible,' said Dennis admiringly. 'I want him drinking at my bar; that moustache alone would entitle him to a free drink. I think a whisky sour, or perhaps a Boulevardier.'

'I think he should…'

'Oh, shut up, Joyce,' scolded Ginger. 'Can't you just admit you like Mark? You'd defend him with your life if someone turned on him.'

Dennis laughed. 'Well, I've found my new in-house entertainment. Hinge and Bracket, eat your hearts out.'

Ginger thumped him on the shoulder.

'Go and fetch dessert, before I set Joyce on you.'

17

*J*oyce typically didn't eat desserts, but after allowing herself to indulge in a gingerbread crème brûlée, she followed Ginger towards their room. As they were about to leave the bar, a retired colonel straight from the pages of an Agatha Christie novel entered. This could only be one person – Mr Dalrymple.

She tapped Ginger on the shoulder. 'I'll catch up with you.'

Marmaduke Dalrymple's smart tweed jacket was worn over a beige V-neck sweater and white-collared shirt. His tie was perfectly straight and his shoes were clearly polished on a daily basis. The look was completed by trousers held in position by a crease sharp enough to do harm if you rubbed against it.

'Half a shandy, if you don't mind.' As he gave his order to bar manager Lisa, Mr Dalrymple hoisted himself up onto a barstool with a little difficulty. Joyce took the seat next to him.

'It's the ideal afternoon to stay in and enjoy a drink,' she said, indicating the dark skies outside the window behind the bar.

'Can't disagree, can't disagree.'

'Is Mrs Dalrymple not joining you?'

He looked surprised. 'No, she likes to have a quick nap after lunch. Do I know you?'

'No, we've not met, but I heard your name in passing. Joyce Brocklehurst.' He shook the hand she offered. He was the kind of gentleman who would never be caught ogling a woman, but even he, Joyce noticed, couldn't resist a quick 'up and down' glance at the vision next to him. Joyce didn't mind; it seemed to be the instinctive response of all men, gay or straight, and a fair few women too when they first laid eyes on her. They just couldn't help it. 'Are you regular guests?'

'Yes, very. We have family in Buxton and as a result we spend a great deal of time here.'

'You prefer your own space, though?'

'What makes you say that?'

'Well, you are close enough to your family to spend a lot of time with them, which would indicate they are equally fond of you and would welcome you into their home for overnight stays. So unless they don't have room, you prefer to stay here – not out of a desire to avoid them, but simply to have some breathing space.'

He smiled at her assessment, delivered in her best 'lady of the manor' voice. She felt he'd respond well to polished enunciation.

'Exactly. We love our son and his family dearly, but he came to fatherhood rather late in life so our grandchildren are very young and energetic, and *we* are rather old.' He even spoke like an Agatha Christie colonel; nothing was clipped, but he seemed to take pleasure in each word and sound.

'And this is the perfect place to tuck yourself away.' Joyce looked around the room; she'd be very happy to tuck herself away here on a regular basis too. Assuming that the dead body in the room was a one-off. 'It's really quite delightful, and the staff are superb.'

'My wife says they are like extended family. I think that's taking it a little too far, but yes, they deliver first-class service, and with plenty of personality too. I like that, even if some of the decor is a little... unusual. Aren't you going to join me?'

Joyce hadn't planned on drinking until cocktail hour struck, but it felt appropriate. She ordered a glass of Californian sparkling wine.

'It must have hit you quite hard if you know the staff so well.'

'What's that?'

'Caroline's death.'

A cloud travelled across his face, and then stayed put. Joyce wasn't sure if it was anger or grief.

'Indeed. A tragic and pointless loss of life. Marjorie was very upset, we both were. An extremely intelligent young lady.' It didn't escape Joyce's attention that as soon as she mentioned Caroline, he stopped looking her in the eye.

'Did you know her particularly well?'

He paused.

'I suppose you'd say we had a business relationship of sorts. Staying here as often as we do, we had the opportunity to chat frequently.'

'You saw one of her talks?'

'Many times, she was extremely knowledgeable. We booked her for a few private tours when we had guests with us. Did you know her?' Joyce couldn't tell from his tone if he was curious or suspicious.

'No, but I've heard so much about her since I arrived, and all of it extremely positive, that I feel as if I do. Perhaps she had something rather troubling going on in her life. If this wasn't an accident, and that's the impression the police are giving, then perhaps she was involved in something and the poor woman needed help.'

'Only the wearer knows where the shoe pinches.' He turned to watch Lisa and took a large drink of the lager shandy he had ordered. Joyce couldn't quite work him out. He was either trying his hardest to avoid the subject of Caroline's murder, or his impeccable manners meant that he found the subject distasteful. As she took a moment to assess him, she couldn't help but notice that despite his advancing years, his slim, bony hands actually looked rather strong.

'You're quite right. We all have our own secrets and mysteries.'

Mr Dalrymple turned back to face her. 'And what are yours?'

Joyce laughed, attempting to sound like a nervous lady who was mildly embarrassed by his question. In reality, she just wanted to grab his boring brown tie and give him a shake.

'Oh, I don't have any secrets, what you see is what you get. A glass of wine, a nice hotel, that's all I need in life.'

Mr Dalrymple gave her another very brief once-over.

'I don't believe that for a minute,' he declared.

18

Ginger knew what Joyce was up to and was pleased to leave Mr Dalrymple in her hands. She knew him as a rather stiff old type. As far as she was aware, he'd never spent a day of his life in the military, but you'd have thought he'd been an admiral or something, the way he wandered round with a stick up his you know what. But, he could also be extremely courteous in an old-fashioned way that Ginger rather missed. She wasn't convinced that he could be charmed by anyone, but if there was one person who might be able to get somewhere, it was Joyce. Either that or she'd beat information out of him with one of her stilettos.

Ginger smiled at that assessment, which was made even funnier because it was true. She knew that Joyce had used that particular form of fashion-based violence on more than one unsuspecting male. Ginger also knew that Joyce and Mr Dalrymple would be undisturbed as Marjorie Dalrymple was well known for her after-lunch naps, leaving her husband to have a drink. They probably needed the space after decades of marriage.

This was why Ginger was particularly surprised to walk into Mrs Dalrymple as she came around the corner. Bundled up in a smart navy-blue coat, the woman had an umbrella in her hand which she dropped as her shoulder came into contact with Ginger's.

'Sorry, sorry.' Mrs Dalrymple grabbed for her umbrella. 'I do apologise. I just saw a break in the rain and decided to go for a walk. Got to be on the safe side, though.' She held the umbrella high, smiled at Ginger and strode as quickly as she could, which was actually more of a slow lurch, towards the door.

Ginger watched her go. Logically, Mrs Dalrymple could do whatever she wanted. She might vary her routine and most people would be none the wiser, but Ginger still found her behaviour rather unusual. Mrs Dalrymple also seemed to be in quite a rush. Her interest piqued, Ginger knew that if she was quick, she could grab her coat and follow the woman. The proverbial doddery old lady, she wasn't going to get very far very quickly.

Mrs Dalrymple was easy to spot, making her way slowly across the Pavilion Gardens. There had been a fresh downpour of rain over lunch and sections of the path were flooded. What light made it through the clouds added a sparkle to the water; although it was a distinctly grey day, there was a pleasant fresh-ness to the air and Ginger was glad that she'd had reason to venture outside. She enjoyed exploring the Derbyshire country-side on foot and was fit, in a hearty kind of a way, as a result.

As she followed the old lady, she considered her possible motivations. There was probably a very simple explanation for why Mrs Dalrymple wasn't taking one of her famous naps and had instead sneaked out of the hotel. Sneaking was what it looked like; she hadn't stopped off at the bar to let her husband know where she was going, but with her slow, slightly lopsided gait, the old woman did look like she was just out for a walk.

Perhaps she had been unable to sleep; she needed some fresh air; she wanted to spend time exploring Buxton on her own. All of these were reasonable assumptions. The rather menacing clouds overhead looked ready to dump rain on the town all over again at any moment, but they weren't far from the hotel and Mrs Dalrymple had brought an umbrella. The more she thought about it, the more Ginger saw nothing unusual in the old woman's actions.

Feeling a little foolish, Ginger slowed down, and then cursed herself as her foot sank into a puddle up to her ankle. The water was cold and made her suck in her breath. Her tights were now wringing wet.

Bother.

She held on to a noticeboard as she took her shoe off and poured water out of it. As she secured her shoe back on and cursed her own stupidity again, Ginger looked up just in time to see a woman waving at Mrs Dalrymple. She looked pleased and a little surprised to see her. After wiping it down with tissues the second woman had pulled out of her pocket, they sat together on a bench and started chatting.

Ginger recognised her: it was Helen Weeks, the head of housekeeping at the hotel. No wonder she was surprised to see Mrs Dalrymple; she would have known her afternoon nap routine as well as anyone. After a couple of minutes, Helen got up and started towards the hotel. She had the right idea; Ginger's foot was uncomfortable, and the enjoyment of getting some fresh air had quickly been soured by the cold creeping up her leg and into the rest of her body. She needed to get her shoes off; maybe even a hot bath was in order. Baths were a great place to think, and she and Joyce hadn't really found any solid clues to work on. Not yet. They were fiddling at the edges of the mystery and it was time to develop a plan. And to develop a plan, Ginger needed a deep, hot bath and an inordinate amount of bubbles.

She took a final look at Mrs Dalrymple. The woman looked

very much at peace with the world, watching some ducks as they wandered past and a small child who was leaping in and out of puddles with squeals of glee. There was nothing to be gained by staying here, so Ginger set off back to the hotel, cringing every time her wet foot hit the ground.

'here are you?' Joyce walked through the adjoining sitting room and into Ginger's bedroom. 'You in here?'

'I'm taking a bath, can't a girl get a moment's peace?'

'It's two o'clock in the afternoon, what on earth are you doing in the bath?'

'Thinking,' came the answer, to which Joyce responded with a huff.

'You're going to come out looking like a prune if you're in there too long. I can't imagine that'll come easy to you.'

'Shut up and get in here. Don't worry, there are plenty of bubbles.'

Joyce was already opening the door. She'd never been shy and she had no reason to believe that Ginger was either; she viewed Ginger as the sort of woman who would walk around a gym changing room naked and not give a stuff about the looks she was getting from women half her age and size. Joyce, on the other hand, wouldn't be seen dead anywhere that didn't have its own constant supply of fresh, hot and fluffy gowns.

Having said that, would Ginger ever go to a gym? Highly unlikely, was Joyce's immediate conclusion.

The roll-top bath that held Ginger was in the middle of the room. The floor was made up of large black-and-white tiles, while all four walls were covered in tiles of a deep burgundy red. As she turned her attention to the occupant of the bath, Joyce was confronted with a red-faced Ginger. Her hair had been shoved unceremoniously onto the top of her head with a couple of pins, but they weren't particularly successful and tendrils stuck to her damp face and neck. A mountain of bubbles covered her body. She'd made two peaks that sat over her breasts.

Joyce sat on the toilet lid. 'Well, they're not right,' she said, staring at the two peaks. Ginger looked at them, slightly confused. 'Shouldn't they be somewhere down each side?' Joyce snorted at her own joke. Ginger threw a handful of bubbles at her, but they fell apart and landed on the floor before they reached her.

'So, did you manage to charm anything of use out of Mr Dalrymple?'

'Not exactly. He didn't tell me anything useful, but he's hiding something, I know he is. He clearly realised I was trying to get information from him, but he wouldn't confront me about it. I think he decided to let our conversation play out, see if he could work out what I was up to.'

'That all sounds a bit complicated. Maybe he doesn't know anything and he was just being polite.'

Joyce wasn't really listening. 'I'm going to have to be careful around him now. Maybe you could try talking to him.'

'Righty-o, I can do that.'

Joyce reached for the makeup bag by the sink and started going through it. Out of the corner of her eye, she caught Ginger watching with amusement as Joyce's lip curled each time she pulled out another tube or tub. Startled by how quickly she ran out of things to examine, she came to the conclusion that Ginger must be a light packer when it came to toiletries. None of the items were brands Joyce had heard of; once again, she was mildly irritated that Ginger seemed to take so little interest in matters of beauty, yet if you looked beyond her over-fondness for comfort, she was rather beautiful.

'If you're short of something to do, you can scrub my back.'

'You should be so lucky. How long have you been in there anyway? Relaxing while I endure the company of Mr Beige.'

'While you were tucked up in the warmth of the bar, glass in hand, I was out in the gardens following Mrs Dalrymple. I climbed in here five minutes before you arrived.'

That got Joyce's attention. 'Why on earth were you following her? Wasn't she having a nap?'

'Is that what her husband told you? Yes, that's what she normally does, everyone knows it. But not this time. She went out for a walk. Last I saw of her, she was saying hello to Helen Weeks who was on her way to work.'

'Who?'

'Helen Weeks, the head of housekeeping here.'

'You didn't stick with her? Mrs Dalrymple, I mean.'

'Where do you think she was going? No, there was nothing to be gained from hiding behind trees, only to follow her back here ten minutes later. Or at least, that's what I assume would have happened. And anyway, I got a bit damp and needed to warm up, hence my afternoon dip.' Ginger turned the hot water tap on with her toe and slipped a little further into the water. Joyce envied her, but decided that while she had a captive audience, she was going to take control.

'Right, let's take this seriously. We've got one dead woman who spent most of her time emulating Mary, Queen of Scots and talking about local history. She was dedicated, hard-working, passionate about her research, but didn't seem to have a lot of friends, if you discount her study buddy. We've got a nice hotel where people return on a regular basis and feel safe enough to have their affairs here. We've also got items missing from people's rooms.

'I think we've got a couple of angles we can look at this from. Maybe Caroline knew who was stealing from the rooms; perhaps she was blackmailing the bloke having the affair; maybe she knows what Mr Dalrymple wasn't telling me. Maybe there's something in her research that someone didn't want getting out.' Ginger started to sit up. 'Stay where you are! I don't need the full show, I've not long had my lunch.' Joyce handed her a towel, averted her eyes and kept talking. 'None of it sounds very convincing. We've just been playing at this, we need more.'

'So what do you suggest?'

'Hopefully we'll find out more from Mark when he gets back to us about Caroline's notes. In the meantime, I want to talk to this head housekeeper you saw with Mrs Dalrymple. You know her?'

'To pass the time of day with.'

'Right, time to stop lounging around, my girl. We have people to interrogate.'

Ginger, who was now standing in the bath wrapped in a towel, grabbed another off a rail and flicked it at Joyce.

'Yes, Sergeant Major. Now bugger off and I'll get dressed.'

20

*a*fter Ginger had dried herself off and opted for a pair of comfortable drawstring trousers, a pale pink polo-neck sweater and a soft grey knee-length cardigan which always made her feel like she was wrapped in a hug, she and Joyce went on a hunt for Helen. They found her inside a linen closet adding towels to a shelf. Ginger wondered briefly how much fun it would be to pull every towel off the shelves and throw herself onto them, especially if they were still warm.

'Ginger, lovely to see you back again. It's been a while for sure.' Helen kept working as she talked. She had the air of a woman who never slowed down. Her hair was scraped back off her face in a utilitarian ponytail, while her bony figure was covered in the housekeeping uniform of black trousers and smock.

'I didn't see you over Christmas when I visited.'

'No, Dennis was good enough to let me 'ave time off. I didn't think I'd get it, but my brother is in Canada and he offered to fly me over. Dennis said he could cope. Anyway, how can I help you ladies? Need more towels?' She turned to face them with a pair of towels draped across her arms.

'No, thank you, we wanted a quick word. Sorry, this is Joyce.'

'Hello, Joyce. Can we talk as I work? I want to get everything set up for the end of the week, I have a to-do list as long as me arm.'

Ginger leant against the door frame. 'We wondered what you could tell us about the thefts from the rooms.'

'Dennis said you might want to have a word about that. Not a lot to tell, really, we had a range of stuff go missing. We spoke to the staff, cracked down on things like tracking master keys and making sure people were signing them in and out. We looked at the rotas to see who was around, but there was no pattern; it wasn't necessarily the same staff on duty each time. Shame really, that would have made things easier.'

'When was the last time it happened?'

Helen looked up at Joyce. 'Month or so ago. A couple of phones went missing.'

'And you have no idea who could be doing it? No suspicions?'

Helen stood to face them. 'Despite all the checkin' I did at the time and the changes we made, I don't want to even imagine that one of my team could be doing it. I don't believe any of them have got it in them. We're not the only team with access to the rooms. Almost anyone on staff could get in if they wanted. I'm sorry, ladies, I really do have a lot to be gettin' on with.'

'Just one more quick question. I saw you speak to Mrs Dalrymple just after lunch in the Pavilion Gardens. Was she alright?'

Helen looked surprised momentarily, and then smiled.

'Oh yes, she's a love. I sat with her for a few minutes on the way here, just to pass the time of day.'

'It's a bit unusual, isn't it?' asked Ginger. 'She normally takes a nap around that time.'

'A bit, but I've seen her get some air before her nap a couple of times. Not often, but it does happen.'

Ginger was about to thank Helen and turn to go, but Joyce spoke first.

'Do you have a son called Ed?'

'I do, yes, works here as well. Why?'

'Just wondered, I recognised the surname. Nice boy, carried our bags for us.'

'He is. Works hard. This place has made him grow up.'

Joyce nodded. 'Thank you.'

'What was that about Ed?' Ginger asked as they walked down the corridor and out of Helen's hearing range.

'Like I said, I spotted his surname. It was on his nametag. I spotted something else as well.' Ginger remained quiet. 'I spotted a bloody big watch on his wrist, one of those things that James Bond and scuba divers wear.' Joyce gave Ginger a look that she interpreted as *how about that, then?*

'Are you saying Ed nicked it?'

'He's hardly likely to wear something that he stole from here, but he might have sold the stolen goods and used the money to buy himself a new watch. His mother could easily cover for him.'

Ginger paused and turned to Joyce. 'But she said that no one member of staff was working every day that something went missing.'

'She's his mother, and she's the head of housekeeping. She's in an ideal position to change the paperwork to make it look like he wasn't working.'

Ginger thought about it. She'd crossed paths with Helen over the years as a guest, but didn't know her well; she had no idea what she was capable of. What Joyce said made sense, but she wasn't sure of one thing.

'What's this got to do with Caroline?'

'If Caroline found out Ed was the thief, then Helen would

want to defend her son. Maybe Helen killed her to prevent her from exposing his criminal tendencies.'

'Or Ed killed her,' Ginger suggested.

'I doubt it, that boy looked terrified of his own shadow. I'm amazed he didn't cause a sonic boom, the speed with which he left our room.' Ginger thought that Joyce could probably terrify the bravest of hearts, but remained silent as her friend carried on speaking. 'No, I don't think he did it, but his mother might have had a good motive.'

21

'So, what's next? You have a plan?'

Joyce was admiring Dennis's bow tie as he spoke: pink with yellow dots. There was no doubt bow ties were old-fashioned, but she still felt it was a shame they were no longer popular. Ginger and Joyce had squeezed into Dennis's office, one of the two rooms behind the reception desk, the chatter of guests drifting in from the lobby. It could easily fit himself and one other, but with the three of them, it was a bit cramped.

'I want to talk to the businessman you said stays here on a regular basis,' she replied. 'John? Can you tell us where he works?'

Dennis sucked air in between his teeth. 'One of the reasons guests like coming here is because they know we respect their privacy. I can't give you personal information. If you get chatting to him while he's here, fine, you're just another guest, but beyond that, I do need to play by the rules.'

'Having us sniffing around is hardly playing by the rules.'

'Very true, Joyce, but that can't get in the way of the service we offer our guests.'

'Okay, can you tell me this: did he ever go on one of Caroline's tours?'

'Not that I'm aware of. I saw them chatting a few times, but then she spoke to most of our guests at one time or another, so it wasn't unusual.'

'You said it would be alright if we ran into him?'

'Of course, I can hardly have anything to do with that, can I?'

Joyce put on her sweetest smile. 'So, I wonder, where might that happen?'

There was silence, until Dennis exclaimed, 'Oh! Oh! You're after a clue, where he might…'

'Come on, Dennis,' Ginger laughed, 'I thought you were quicker than that. She wasn't even being very subtle.'

'I'd be amazed if she knew how to do subtle. Look, I don't want to lose a regular guest or put my reputation at risk.' Dennis was the only one sitting and the two women towered over him. Joyce knew he would weaken, it was only a matter of time, so she remained looking at him, not blinking.

'Oh, for heaven's sake. I believe he's rather fond of a bar called Wine Down. Get it? *Wind down*? Well, it's up on George Street. He often takes clients in there and I've spotted him a couple of times myself. That's all I'm telling you.'

Joyce leant over and kissed him on the cheek. There was a degree of delight at the size of the lipstick mark she left behind. As she stood up, Ginger went to wipe it off, but Joyce stopped her with a look. The idea of him carrying on his day utterly unaware of the glorious imprint of lips that now glowed on his cheek gave her immense satisfaction. Ginger grinned back at her.

'What? What are you two up to?'

'Nothing, dearest,' Ginger replied. 'Nothing.'

The two women wandered out of the hotel. They were in no rush as they didn't expect John to be at the bar, especially late on a Sunday afternoon. The chances were that he had gone home to his wife, but they were curious and didn't have anything else to do.

'Well, you're back at work tomorrow, so we're going to have a lot less time to work on this.'

Joyce looked surprised by Ginger's comment. 'I'm going nowhere. I'm owed some time off, it's not busy. Oh yes, and I'm the boss.'

'Of the shops, not the whole place. Don't get above yourself. Won't you need to tell the Duke and Duchess?'

Joyce thought about the Duke and Duchess of Ravensbury, her employers. Unless they had a meeting scheduled with her, they never knew from one day to the next what she was doing.

'Not at all. So long as things are running smoothly, which they *always* are, they won't even notice. They have my mobile number if they want me. I'm going to stay here and work this out. Regardless of what Dennis says, we need to find that John Bradbury and talk to him as quickly as possible. I'd also like to find out what the police know so far, but I'm not sure how we'll get that information.'

Ginger appeared to be only half listening. 'What's it like, working for a Duke and Duchess?'

'It's like working for anyone else, but they've got a very personal interest in everything. It's their home and family that we're talking to the public about after all. But they're very down to earth, or as down to earth as it's possible to get with a 300-room house and 40,000-acre estate; they're not all airs and graces.'

'Don't you ever cross swords with the Duchess?'

'Why on earth would I do that?'

'Well, let's be honest, you're hardly shy and retiring yourself. I can imagine the two of you coming to blows over the exact amount of gold leaf that should adorn a trinket box, or whether selling socks with the faces of the Duke and Duchess on them lowers the tone of the shops.'

'We wouldn't argue over that because they *would* lower the tone, and she'd know that I was right, and she'd never suggest it anyway.' Ginger peered at her out of the corner of her eye. 'Don't look at me like that. She's wise enough to leave me to it. I look after the shop, make them a healthy profit which increases year on year, and they pop in to say hello from time to time. There are other parts of the business that need their attention a lot more and they trust me.'

'At least they will until the day you start selling a calendar of "hot dukes", with the Duke of Ravensbury making an appearance as Lord July.'

'I wouldn't dream of doing anything so tacky.' She had, but Joyce wasn't going to tell Ginger that.

22

*J*oyce and Ginger walked past the honey coloured arches of the Georgian townhouses, turning right as they reached the Opera House with its posters for The Hollies tribute band that was playing that evening, and along a narrow backstreet.

'The chances of him being there just after Dennis has told us about it are pretty much zero,' Ginger said, 'but at least we can take a look, check out the kind of place he likes to go for a drink.'

They stopped outside Wine Down and peered through the window. It was an expensive-looking place with racks of wine behind glass covering the walls from floor to ceiling. Black leather and dark wood sucked out any light that made its way in; Ginger wondered if that was to convince drinkers it was later than it actually was and therefore encourage them to start drinking earlier.

She knew some people were intimidated by places like this, but not her. The owners were probably up to their necks in debt and just trying to keep the place afloat; it was a challenging business to get into. There were about a dozen drinkers scattered around. The young man behind the bar, wearing a black t-shirt and trilby, was paying a lot of attention to two women around the same age as he was, so she wasn't at much risk of being spotted.

'Want to go in?' Ginger asked.

'No. I don't need a drink.'

Ginger took a second look, and then cupped her hands against the window.

'Stop it.' Joyce nudged her hard. 'That's too obvious.'

'Well, you might want a drink now.'

Joyce turned and peered through the glass. 'What am I looking at?'

'Behind the bar, mid-thirties, long brown hair. White shirt. I'm sure I've seen her somewhere…' She tried to think where she knew the woman from. A couple of guests had been checking out as they arrived, or maybe she had been walking past the hotel.

Joyce was more certain. 'Well spotted. I've seen her at the hotel, she was with John Bradbury. We haven't found our man, but we have found his woman.' The subject of their interest had been pulling on her coat as she appeared behind the bar and was now heading for the door. Joyce and Ginger turned round and pretended to be deep in conversation.

'…I told her he was as much use as a chocolate teapot, and he just went and proved me right, but you know what she's like.' Ginger was trying very hard to sound natural, while Joyce was nodding wildly in exaggerated agreement.

'You are so right, it's like I told our Betty. *Marriage is like a game of cards. To begin with you need two hearts and a diamond. By the end, you just wish you had a club and a spade.*'

'Aye,' Ginger agreed, 'couldn't 'ave put it better myself.'

Out of the corner of her eye she watched the woman walk past and, with some relief, saw that she was taking no notice of the two gossips standing outside the bar.

'Come on,' she whispered to Joyce, 'let's follow her.'

The woman seemed to be retracing the route they had just

walked from The Lodge. She was typing a text message as she went and Ginger wondered how long it would be until she walked into a lamppost or tripped on a kerb. Despite the woman's preoccupation with her phone, Ginger was still concerned they'd get spotted. It didn't matter how many shadowy doorways she ducked in and out of, being with someone who dressed the way Joyce did was like carrying a sign which said *look at us, we're following you.*

It didn't take them long to find out where the woman was going. They rounded the corner beyond the Old Hall Hotel, past the Buxton Visitor Centre in the old Pump Room and the grand sweep of a beautiful Georgian crescent which had been beautifully restored and was now home to the rather fancy Crescent Hotel. They watched her go into the door of the Royal Spa, which did exactly what it said on the tin. It was one of the town's most modern and expensive spas.

'Well, that explains that,' declared Ginger.

'Want to enlighten me?'

'The shirt she was wearing had a logo on it. She works here. She must have two jobs. That'll make you very happy.'

'Overjoyed.' They stood in silence before Joyce asked, 'Precisely what am I overjoyed about?'

'Because tomorrow, we're going to have a luxurious spa treatment, all in the name of identifying a killer.'

Joyce did look pleased. Ginger on the other hand was less excited. The last time she'd been for a spa treatment was... well, never. She had no idea what she was in for.

23

*J*oyce pushed her empty plate to the side and pulled out her phone.

'Am I not good enough?' Ginger asked as she finished her fish and chips, or rather a fancy version that looked like giant fish fingers served in newspaper covered in fictional Buxton news made especially for The Lodge.

'What?' Joyce didn't raise her eyes.

'Am I such dull company that you need to start scrolling through that thing?'

Joyce turned the phone so Ginger could see what she was looking at. It was the website for the Royal Spa.

'I'm browsing the staff profiles and… there she is. Lydia Foyle.' She clicked on the phone number on the screen. 'Oh hello, I was wondering if Lydia Foyle is working tomorrow? A friend has recommended her… Marvellous. I'd like to make a reservation for myself and a friend at 2pm…Swedish massage for myself and a facial and pedicure for…yes that's right…Looking forward to it… Thank you ever so much.' Joyce ended the call and turned to Ginger. 'There. Let's see how chatty Ms Foyle is.'

'Ladies, how is dinner?' Dennis loomed over them and Joyce

noted that the handkerchief in his top pocket matched the pink and yellow bow tie she'd been admiring earlier.

'Yummy,' declared Ginger as she cleaned her plate with a piece of bread. 'Can you join us?'

'I was hoping you'd say that.' He caught the eye of a server and twirled his finger over the table. 'I fancy the fish and chips myself. So, how has your day been? Finding time to relax?'

'If you consider following people and thinking about nothing but murder relaxing, then sure,' answered Ginger.

'Don't give me that, Ginger Salt, you're not the type to lounge around having spa treatments or reading romcoms by the pool. Come to think of it, I don't think you've ever been to a spa in your life.'

'*WHAT?*' Joyce wondered if she'd heard right. 'Never... spa... not once... what the...?'

'Keep your wig on, old girl. So I've never been to a spa; I'm not sure it means my life has been devoid of purpose.'

'Oh, I don't know about that. Well, tomorrow is going to be a momentous occasion and I'm in charge. I will make sure you have an afternoon to remember.'

'Does this mean what I think it means?' asked Dennis, not taking his eyes off Ginger as he sat back to allow a server to lay a place in front of him.

'Yes, sort of, but it's still in the name of investigating a murder, so don't get too excited.

'You need to explain.'

'It turns out that John Bradbury's mistress works at the bar you told us about, so I'm guessing that's how they met, but she also has a second job at the Royal Spa. Joyce has booked us in and we're going to see if we can get anything out of her – if she ever got to know Caroline, saw anything suspicious. Maybe Caroline had issues with their illicit relationship.'

'I doubt that was an issue, Caroline never gave me any indication that she had a problem with what they were doing. But at least this way, you might not have to talk to John and risk damaging his relationship with the hotel. Then again, Lydia might report your conversation straight back to John, so you still need to be careful.'

'Oh, we will, don't worry. We can be very subtle.'

Both Dennis and Ginger turned to stare at Joyce, who decided not to dignify their reaction with a response.

'While you're here, Dennis, could we pick your brain about two of your staff?' she asked instead. Dennis looked around the room before answering Joyce's question.

'You may. Who do you want to know about?'

'Helen and Ed. I know they're mother and son, but tell us more.'

'Helen has been with us for years. Her mother had the job before her, and her grandmother before that, so they're very much part of The Lodge family. Helen is hard-working, knows a lot of the returning guests well. Come Christmas, she has a stack of gifts from many of them. Mr and Mrs Dalrymple are a prime example, they treat her like extended family. Helen's daughter isn't following in her footsteps, though; she's a hairdresser in Macclesfield. Ed joined us two years ago, give or take.'

'He seems a bit wet to me. Is he any good?'

'He's a teenage boy. If he didn't still live with his mother, I'm sure he'd turn up late and look like he'd been dragged through a hedge backwards, but that would never happen under Helen's watch. He's polite with the guests, does as he's told; he sometimes needs a bit of encouragement, has his sullen days like all lads his age, but he's decent overall.'

'Is this his only job?' Ginger asked, stealing a chip off the plate that had just been placed in front of Dennis.

'No, he also works at Treetops; he juggles the two jobs and his college work. Something else that is only possible because of Helen, I'm sure.'

Ginger nodded, but Joyce was in the dark.

'And Treetops is?'

'One of those adventure places where you climb rope bridges in the trees, balance along branches and whiz down zip lines. All rather energetic for my liking, but it's hugely popular.'

Joyce was gobsmacked. 'The boy's got the physique of a pipe cleaner. How come he's not got muscles the size of a small country?'

'I can only assume that the lack of meat on his bones means there isn't a great deal of weight for him to have to cart around.'

'Is it well paid?'

'I have no idea, why?'

'Because he's wearing a watch that wouldn't give him much change out of £500. Based on your description of Helen, I imagine her frowning on such an extravagant purchase and I'm wondering how he can afford it.'

'He's hardly likely to wear it here if he nicked it from a guest,' Ginger reiterated before Dennis could respond.

'True, but it's enough to cast suspicion on him.'

While Dennis tucked in to his fish and chips, Joyce took her chance.

'Now, while I've got you here, Dennis, I want some information from you.'

'Oh yes?' he mumbled. 'Should I have a lawyer present?'

'I want all the juicy gossip on Ginger's love life. She's been far too quiet about it all, but I have no doubt that Derbyshire is riddled with broken hearts.' Joyce didn't miss the pleading look that Ginger gave him over her glass. 'Come on, I'm convinced she's been engaged at least once, and I wouldn't be surprised if there's a marriage somewhere in the shadows.'

'Well...' Dennis slowly dabbed at each corner of his mouth with a napkin. 'She's had no shortage of offers, but try as I might, she keeps on declining every temptation I have placed in her way...'

Joyce's phone chimed and Ginger mock wiped sweat from her brow.

'A narrow escape *this time,* Salt. It's Mark, says he's onto the last notebook and wonders if we fancy a nightcap later. He'll talk us through what he's found in Caroline's research.'

'Good.' Ginger looked relieved. 'That was quick. The sooner we can get them back off him and hand them to Harnby, the better. We'll be in a lot of trouble if she goes to find Madeleine and discovers we held on to them.'

24

Ginger was always pleased to see Mark. He was polite, beautifully dressed, full of incredible snippets of information – he was able to absorb details like a sponge. Best of all, he could give Joyce as good as she delivered. It was like watching two siblings fight like cat and dog, knowing all along that each was the other's fiercest protector.

Having said that, there were times when it got tiresome and Ginger wished they'd just pack it in and behave like grownups. Hopefully this evening Joyce would play nicely, seeing as Mark had clearly been working hard all afternoon doing them a favour. As soon as he'd arrived, they'd returned to the Stanage Suite, Dennis promising to be along shortly with drinks. He was as keen to hear what Mark had discovered as Joyce and Ginger were.

'Not bad, not bad at all.' Mark looked around the room, taking in the turquoise carpet and the vast mirror in the heavy gold frame which sat opposite the painting of Stanage Edge. He made himself comfortable in the rich blue armchair and put Caroline's notes in a pile on the coffee table, moving a bell jar with a bright orange butterfly in it to one side. Joyce and Ginger sat on the sofa, looking oddly uncomfortable. In fact, Ginger was trying to control herself and was one step away from bouncing up and down in her seat like an impatient child. For her part, Joyce looked as though she was holding back from shouting out the million sarcastic comments that were likely to be ricocheting around inside her head. Ginger imagined what a few of them might be as Mark fiddled with the end of his moustache while they waited for Dennis to appear.

'You both owe Bill a drink or two. He was hoping for a date at the cinema and a nice pub meal for dinner. Instead, he went to the cinema on his own like Billy No-mates.'

'You've got yourself a good 'un there,' Ginger said firmly. 'Keep your mitts on him.'

'Don't worry, I will. As it happens, he managed to help me with a bit of this before he left.' Mark tapped the top of the pile of notebooks.

'Sorry I took so long.' Dennis swung open the door. He was out of breath and pushing a trolley with four glasses and a bottle of bourbon. 'Joyce, here's your Brandy Alexander; Mark, you and I have got Old Fashioneds; Ginger… I just brought you the bottle and some ice. You'll still be more steady on your feet than the lot of us. I swear you've got hollow legs.'

Ginger blew him a kiss as he pulled up the desk chair and joined the circle of furniture around the coffee table.

'Thank you, darlin'. You know how to treat your guests. Now that we're all here, the stage is yours, Mr Boxer.'

Mark took a drink, and then made a start.

'Okay, so, a lot of this is as you'd expect. Caroline was continuing to do research on Mary, Queen of Scots and getting ready for the new season. My guess is she was very much a passionate amateur who wanted to take it up a notch, and as a result she was working towards her Blue Badge. That's the sort of official qualification for British tour guides, it's how you can tell you've got the real deal. I have one. Caroline was extending her research into more Buxton-specific topics so she could expand her walking tours around the town, covering more of its history, although Mary was clearly her main interest.'

Mark reached for a notebook on the top of the pile. 'It starts to get interesting here, though. Caroline was researching the Well Women.'

Ginger had no idea what he was talking about; Joyce and Dennis looked equally blank. Mark seemed to pick up on this.

'So, in 1772, there was something called the Enclosures Act. In that, it ruled that Buxton's natural spring water should always be freely available to the town's residents. The source – the well – needed to be looked after, kept clean and in good repair. Well Women were appointed every Easter for the year ahead. These women were poor – they were unpaid and depended on tips – but of good character.

'There are a couple of famous ones: Martha Brandreth, who died at the age of eighty-one in 1795. And Martha Norton did the job fifteen times – there are a number of pictures of her at the Buxton Museum. Caroline had come across another woman by the name of Betty Goodrush, who was a Well Woman during a similar period to Martha Norton, although it doesn't look like there are any pictures of her. Or at least, Caroline doesn't make any reference to them. That's something else: Caroline's research seems to be very thorough and there are a lot of reference notes, so I have no reason to believe that everything I'm telling you now isn't based on good evidence that we could access ourselves if we wanted to.'

He paused for another drink. 'Everyone with me so far?' There were nods and murmurs. 'Great. This is the good bit. Caroline obviously spotted something of interest, because the next thing is she's down a genealogical rabbit hole, and what does she discover?'

'Carrots?' suggested Joyce. Dennis laughed, Ginger tried to

stifle a smile and Mark shook his head like a parent used to childish interruptions.

'No, not a source of improved eyesight. Caroline discovered that she is in fact a direct descendant of Betty Goodrush.'

'Goodness me, that's remarkable,' said Dennis. He'd shuffled forward and was sitting on the edge of his seat – dangerously close to the edge, Ginger thought. 'I bet she'd have loved that. She could have used it in one of her tours; I wonder why she didn't say anything.'

'Because there's more to it than that,' Mark said, taking the opportunity for a couple of sips of his Old Fashioned before adding more ice from the bucket. 'Betty Goodrush went missing, and a couple of months later her body was found. She'd been murdered.'

---

25

*J*oyce had remained silent while Mark was speaking and she wasn't about to interrupt him now, but even she was having trouble remaining cool, calm and collected. Her thoughts were shooting ahead, trying to work out how this historical murder could be linked to their present-day one. She knew people could maintain a grudge for a long time, a lifetime even, but if anyone were to have a grudge here, it would be Caroline. After all, it had been her ancestor who had been killed.

Joyce watched as Mark hunted for a piece of paper. He was in his element, surrounded by records of the past. Stick him in a library and lock the door and he wouldn't complain. He wouldn't need food; he didn't look like he ate much anyway. Mind you, Joyce knew that wasn't entirely true; he could eat three times as much as her and not put on an ounce. She, on the other hand...

'Joyce... Oi, you paying attention?' Ginger was digging a finger in her side. She was grateful that Ginger didn't possess nails to rival her own.

'What? Yes, he's just got me thinking. Carry on, professor.'

Mark smiled at her and Joyce cursed herself for giving any

clue that what he'd said was interesting. She liked to keep him on his toes.

'There was only limited coverage of Betty's murder in the press. After all, she wasn't anyone significant, and there was no word of the killer being caught. That was it; no one was really interested. Caroline on the other hand clearly wanted to know what had happened to her relative and started to dig around.

'About six months after Betty's murder, a local man, Burn Halpin, was arrested for almost beating someone to death. The reports say that he had a history of a violent temper and was wanted in connection with another crime, but it doesn't say what. The authorities were also looking for another man who was believed to have carried out the attacks with him. My guess is this got Caroline thinking and she followed the trail.'

Mark stopped and drained his glass. He paused.

'For God's sake, someone pour him a drink,' Ginger demanded. 'I don't want him running out of steam now.' Dennis added bourbon and ice to Mark's glass. Mark took a sip before continuing.

'Caroline hit a lot of dead ends. There was no solid evidence to tie Burn Halpin to Betty, and nothing about his possible co-conspirator. Anyway, looking at the dates in her notes, I believe Caroline gave up for a while, and focused back on getting ready for the spring and her qualifying as a Blue Badge Guide.'

He stopped and there was a collective groan around the room.

'That's it?' cried Joyce. 'Bloody hell, Mark Boxer, you do know how to lead a girl on.'

A distinctly cheeky smile crept across Mark's face.

'You didn't find anything else?' Dennis asked before sitting back in his chair. 'That was interesting, but it doesn't seem to have led us anywhere.'

Joyce looked over at Ginger who hadn't moved or said anything. She was staring at Mark, her expression reflecting the small smile on his face.

'What?' demanded Joyce.

'He's having you on,' said Ginger quietly and with a certain amount of glee.

'What do you mean he's… oh, hang on a minute, have you got more? You're a swine, Boxer! Come on, spit it out.'

He laughed. 'I do love winding you up, my dear Joyce, it's so much fun.'

'You won't be having much fun once I get out of this seat.'

'Are they always like this?' Dennis asked Ginger. 'I'm not sure whether to be amused or worried; either way, it's entertaining.'

'They're always like this,' confirmed Ginger. 'Come on, Mark, before the good Lady Brocklehurst bursts a blood vessel.'

'Alright. So, about fifteen years later, our chap with a violent temper makes a deathbed confession. Probably wanted to increase his hopes of getting up to the Pearly Gates, but not much chance of that because he confessed to two murders, one of which was that of Betty Goodrush. This time a second name is attached, William, who Halpin says carried out the attack with him. Sorry, no surname.'

'Is the second murder victim important?' asked Dennis.

'Good question, but Caroline's notes don't say anything about that.'

'And this second man, William, what do we know about him?'

'Nothing. It's as though Caroline ran out of time.'

'Dammit.' Joyce was seriously frustrated. 'I feel like you've just ripped the last page out of a book. So how do we find out more?'

Mark turned the notebook round so they could see.

'This name, I know her. Phyllis Wolfe. She works over at the Visitor Centre and she knows a great deal about the Well Women. I've no doubt that Caroline spoke to her; she may well be able to tell you what they discussed and point you in the right direction so you can pick up the trail for yourselves.'

Joyce sat back in her chair. 'Is that it? It took you all day to work that out?'

Mark didn't rise to the bait. 'You couldn't wade through the first couple of pages on Mary, Queen of Scots without getting frustrated and handing the job over to me. There was a lot of other stuff in there; you'd never have found Betty's story hidden in it. Besides which, I had the laundry to do and my own preparation for a tour I'm delivering at Charleton House tomorrow. You're lucky I could fit this in at all.'

'We're very grateful,' said Ginger. 'We did give up.' She looked at Joyce as she made the final comment.

'Don't worry, I know she loves me. Don't you, Joyce?'

Joyce didn't say anything, her desire to wind Mark up as strong as his to reciprocate. Instead, she topped up his glass and, almost imperceptibly, raised her own to him.

26

*M*ark and Dennis had stayed on with Joyce and Ginger in the Stanage Suite for another couple of hours after the revelation about Caroline and her ancestor, and between the four of them, they'd finished the bottle of bourbon and moved on to the port. Luckily, Bill had been on hand to pick Mark up on his way home from his solo trip to the cinema. While Dennis was the worse for wear, the two women had convinced him to be the one to get the notes to DS Harnby; he would claim that Madeleine had dropped them off at the hotel.

The next morning, Ginger and Joyce were both tired and had breakfast in their room.

'I'm way too old for this malarkey,' Ginger groaned as they got themselves ready to go out. 'It's only Monday and I'm done in.'

'I thought you had hollow legs?' Joyce called through from her bedroom.

'I must have had 'em filled in. There was a time in my life when I could drink anyone under the table and not feel a thing the next day.'

'It's called getting old. It's also called mixing your drinks. You'd have been fine if you hadn't moved on to the port.'

'Oh yeah, I forgot about that.' Ginger groaned to herself; it was a rookie mistake.

'Memory loss is also a sign of old age. Are you ready?'

'Ready, willing and able. As are you – for a shift at the garden centre, by the looks of things.'

Joyce had stepped into the room wearing an outfit which, to Ginger's eyes, made her resemble a pot plant. Tight-fitting brown trousers and brown snakeskin ankle boots were topped off with a bright green jumper. Little bobbles followed the line of the shoulders and down the arms; with only a bit of imagination, they made her resemble a succulent.

'Please tell me you have green reading glasses,' Ginger begged.

'And what if I do?'

'Bloody brilliant! And let me see…' Ginger grabbed Joyce's hands; it was just as she'd expected. Bright green nail polish with a very thin white line down the middle.

'And what is your contribution to the world of fashion?' Joyce asked with what sounded like an air of defensiveness, which Ginger knew wasn't genuine.

'This morning, I am adding sunshine and light to the world. I made this jumper myself.' Joyce examined the bright yellow jumper for a moment, clearly impressed. 'My silver hair is a cloud that suggests rain, but will actually cast a small shadow in order to protect you should my rays become a little too hot.'

'Okay, now you're blathering.'

After picking up her bag, Ginger looked over at Joyce's nails again.

'Careful with those. In a certain light, you might look like you've been picking your nose.' Ginger was still giggling as they left the room.

The Buxton Visitor Centre was less than a minute's walk from the hotel and Ginger made the short journey on her own. Joyce had another appointment in their search for information about Caroline. The building she was heading for had been constructed in 1894 to provide an alternative place for people to 'take the waters', as other locations were becoming overcrowded; another was a drinking well just outside the building where the public would turn up to this day to fill empty bottles. It had recently been renovated and now the elegant room inside was used as a centre where visitors could get information, buy gifts and see where the Well Women would have worked. It was a beautifully elegant space on two levels; you could look down onto one of the locations where the water of St Ann's well appeared and was ladled out into glasses. The well actually resembled a large oval marble bath.

A woman in a pale-blue Edwardian dress with a starched white collar and cuffs and a frilly white apron spotted Ginger.

'You can come on down and take a closer look if you'd like.'

'Thank you,' Ginger replied, 'but I'm looking for Phyllis Wolfe.'

'I'm Clara the Well Woman, but I have been known to go by the name Phyllis, especially when there aren't any school groups around.'

Phyllis had a surprisingly soft voice for someone who worked with schoolchildren; Ginger wondered how she made herself heard and concluded that she must be a pussycat who could suddenly roar like a lion at a terrifying volume if needed. Ginger descended the curved staircase with its curly wrought-iron baluster into the marbled space below. She felt as though she was walking into someone's bathroom in full view of the public; it was a decidedly odd sensation.

'I'm Ginger, Ginger Salt, and I'm hoping you can help me.'

'How can I be of assistance? Take a seat, please.'

Ginger sat on the hard marble shelf that ran either side of the space like a bench.

'I wanted to talk to you about a conversation you had with

Caroline Clatworthy, the woman who was murdered over the weekend.'

'I heard about that, it's terribly sad. So disturbing to think that a killer has been at work so close to where we are. Visitors tend to think that Buxton is such a genteel place, but really we're like any town in England. We have all the usual problems, but even so, you don't imagine that murder would ever be one of them, and certainly not the murder of someone you know.' She said the word *murder* like she was trying it out – a word that she had seldom had reason to utter and was unfamiliar with how it sounded coming from her own mouth. 'Did you know Caroline?'

'Friend of a friend,' replied Ginger. Phyllis nodded slowly.

'Well pass on my condolences to your friend. How is it I can help?'

'I know that you had contact with Caroline recently as she was researching the Well Woman, Betty Goodrush. I was wondering what you could tell me about that.'

'Yes, Caroline was very interested. I believe she discovered a personal link. Betty Goodrush was a lesser-known Well Woman, but important all the same. We helped Caroline with some research here; a number of the team have quite a lot of information on Betty, and she also spent time at the Buxton Museum and Art Gallery. They have some wonderful material there.'

'Did she ever give you any indication that she had found something worrying?'

'You mean Betty's murder? Oh yes, we discussed that. Very sad. Oh, how awful!' Phyllis looked briefly shocked. 'Do you think the two things might be connected?'

'I can't see how, there's over 200 years between the two events. Did anyone else come looking for the same information, or asking about Caroline's research?'

'No, not that I can recall, why would they? This *is* to do with Caroline's murder, isn't it?'

Ginger really hoped that Phyllis did have a sleeping lion

inside, otherwise she was going to be eaten alive by the next batch of schoolchildren.

'No, I'm just trying to get a picture of what she was like, what she was working on.'

'I don't know what else I can tell you. We had a couple of delightful conversations over tea and I asked her to share her research with us. It's such a shame, a dreadful tragedy.'

'Are you able to give me the name of anyone up at the museum who might be able to help?'

'Oh yes, Lewis Ashmore. He's a lovely young man and he'll be able to help you with anything you need. I'm sorry I can't tell you any more.' She looked so genuinely sorry that Ginger felt bad for her.

'You've been a great help, honestly.'

'Oh, I am glad.'

It was lucky their conversation was over as the calm of the space was ruined by the chatter and screams of a school group who had just entered the Visitor Centre. Phyllis stood up and gave herself a shake; an actual physical shake.

'Right then,' she said in the same gentle voice, 'no rest for the wicked. It wa' lovely to meet you, Ginger.' She skipped up the steps. As she reached the top, she paused briefly before projecting her voice with a force that startled Ginger.

'Good morning, children, if you could all gather around me.'

Ginger stared up at her. The lion had roared.

27

*J*oyce had never heard of Robert Rippon Duke, an English architect who, according to Dennis, was responsible for much of Victorian Buxton. She certainly hadn't expected to start the week talking to a man who had been dead for over 100 years, but there seemed to be no limit to how unusual this so-called relaxing break could become.

Duke was one of the historical figures who led tours around part of Buxton. After a couple of phone calls, Dennis had found out that a private tour was taking place that morning. Joyce hoped that the guide would be there early and she could ask him a few questions before he set off with his group of architecture students from Derby University.

The Devonshire Dome building was originally a rather over-the-top set of stables, which at that time had the world's largest free-standing dome. Quite whether the horses paid any attention to the architectural wonder above them is anybody's guess; Joyce assumed they were more interested in their lunch. After housing 120 horses, the building was transformed into the Devonshire Royal Hospital, which made Joyce picture beds in the individual bays of the stables, nurses walking through straw. Not the case, of course. Now it was part of Derby University, and the last time Joyce had visited it was to eat at the restaurant that was run by the catering students. She'd been pleasantly surprised by the high quality of the food, as good as any professional restaurant she'd eaten in. Now, however, she was standing at the edge of the airy space, looking for a man with a large, bushy white beard, wearing a top hat.

The man she was seeking was checking the time on an old-fashioned pocket watch, but he looked up as Joyce approached.

'Dr March?'

'No, Joyce Brocklehurst. I doubt anyone would allow me to operate on them.'

He took in the figure before him and made his own decision. 'I might be prepared to allow you try. But Dr March is the head of the architecture department at the university, so no surgery required. Are you looking for me?'

'If you are Robert Rippon Duke, then I am indeed, and based on your outfit, I'm hoping you are he.'

He removed his top hat and bowed. 'I am he, and I'm honoured to meet you, Ms Brocklehurst. I would find it hard to believe, but are you one of the students?'

Joyce shuddered. 'My student days were never that successful to begin with and certainly not to be repeated.'

He laughed. 'If you're not here to learn about Tuscan Doric pilasters or the involvement of the Cotton Districts Convalescent Fund, how can I help you?'

He walked her to a couple of chairs and waited for her to sit before joining her. Despite his white beard, his walking stick was clearly a prop; he moved like a much younger man with a smooth, long stride. Joyce imagined he was, or had been, a runner, or perhaps a cyclist.

'How can I be of assistance?'

Joyce wasn't sure whether his particularly gentlemanly

approach was genuine or part of his character. Either way, she approved.

'I wanted to talk to you about Caroline Clatworthy.'

He took on a sterner look than seconds ago, but not unfriendly.

'Caroline, yes, that was very sad. Are you a friend?'

'Yes, of a sort.'

'Then you have my condolences. She was a lovely woman. What is it you'd like to know?'

'Did you have much to do with her?'

'Not at this time of year; none of us are very busy. We keep in touch, but really, we're waiting for Easter when the season starts in earnest. Then as things get warmer and busier, there are events, our general bookings go up and we see more of one another. We fundamentally work alone, but our paths do cross.'

'When you did have contact with her recently, did she seem different? Like something was on her mind?'

'No, but we only exchanged a few emails. No more than that.'

'Is it a particularly competitive line of work? Do any of you ever fall out?'

Robert Rippon Duke laughed at that idea. 'We're all far too polite for that. We do get frustrated when unqualified guides come into town and we hear some of the ridiculous things they tell their clients, but at worst, we sit in the pub and complain over a gin and tonic. Are you, I wonder… are you actually asking if there might be enough competition to result in murder?' He raised an eyebrow and stared at her.

'Oh no, that would be ridiculous,' replied Joyce, despite that being exactly what she had been suggesting.

'Good to hear it, it would indeed. Now, I think I can see my group arriving. Can I help with anything else?'

'Did Caroline ever give any indication to you that something was bothering her? That there was something in her life that could lead to trouble?'

'No. But I will say that this winter, she took longer to reply to her emails than usual. It briefly crossed my mind that I had done something to offend her, but she did always reply eventually and I put it down to her being busy. She was certainly distracted, if it's possible to tell that from an email. But beyond that, nothing stands out. Now, if you'll excuse me...' He stood swiftly and offered her his hand, which Joyce accepted as she also stood.

'Thank you for your time.'

'The pleasure was all mine.' He bowed his head, replaced his hat, gave it a sharp tap and strode off. It had been the sort of elegant encounter that Joyce could get used to.

28

Ginger had many happy memories of visiting the Buxton Museum as a child. Her father was fascinated by geology and would take her along to show her the mineral collections. It was the fossils that drew her attention, those and a mermaid which although likely to induce nightmares was something that caught her imagination. Each visit had to start with a viewing.

The exhibit, which appears to be a mummified mermaid, has a small human-like upper body and skull, the lower half being a curved tail. Even now, Ginger thought it was hideous, but this weird fantastic beast was most definitely captivating. Today, however, she entered the Victorian corner building with other thoughts on her mind: the murder of a Well Woman over 200 years ago.

Lewis Ashmore wasn't at all what she was expecting. He looked about twenty-five, wore a grey hoodie and skin-tight jeans, and his hair, which was long enough to hang over his ears, looked as if it needed a good brush. But he welcomed her with a broad smile and a lively *hello there,* and she was immediately charmed in a 'wanting to mother him' kind of way. He took her into a small office with floor-to-ceiling metal bookcases and a heavy wooden desk. She was surprised to find it pristinely tidy, with an open laptop, a single neat pile of papers, and a large thermal coffee mug. She guessed what it held because of the words printed on the mug: *I don't need inspirational quotes, I need coffee.*

'Caroline spent ages here. I dug out everything I could find about Betty, it was fascinating. I was familiar with Martha Brandreth and Martha Norton, but Betty was new to me. Her death was deemed worthy of less than an inch in a newspaper and it was only because Caroline was prepared to scour every newspaper that we found even that. Or rather, she did. It blew my mind when she came back one day and said they were related.'

'What about Betty's killer, Burn, and the deathbed confession?'

'The first evidence Caroline found of that was a piece of second-hand gossip in someone's diary, probably something they had heard down the pub years after Betty's death that became part of local mythology. I did find more, which led me to believe that the reference to Burn was incorrect, certainly in relation to Betty; it's likely that Burn was a murderer, but he didn't kill Betty. The name William, however; that was interesting, as was pulling everything I'd found together for Caroline. I spoke to her on the phone to tell her what I had, but she never came to see it for herself and... well, then I heard she'd been killed.' He looked uncomfortable at that point and reached for his mug. 'Would you like to see it? Would it be helpful?'

'Oh my God, yes, I'd love to.'

Lewis grabbed a folder off the shelf. 'I didn't put this away because I knew Caroline would want to see it. As I said, the original clue came from an 1870s diary which referenced the deathbed confession to a couple of murders from a local man. This is a copy.' The page was covered in tightly packed slanted handwriting. 'There was no evidence to back it up, but it certainly set us off down the right track.'

'When did all this happen?'

'Betty went missing in 1805; she was sixty. She left behind a son and a daughter and a number of grandchildren. Her daughter died not long after. There was no more reference to Betty's death, but the name William was something I thought was worth following up, and I found these.'

He logged in to his laptop and pulled up some photos. They were of old newspaper articles. He turned the computer around so Ginger could read them; he had used some sort of electronic highlighter on one of the photos to mark the relevant paragraph.

Arthur Grover, who calls himself an 'amateur detective', has spent many of his adult years seeking his ancestor's killer. After many hours of diligent work, he has attributed the death to a Mr William Bennett, a tradesman who died in 1834. Mr Grover has discovered that Mr Bennett made a deathbed confession. It is believed that Mr Bennett murdered Septimus Grover over an unpaid bill. A Well Woman who disappeared in 1805 is believed to be another of Mr Bennett's victims and anyone with further information is encouraged to come forward.

'Where did you find this?'

'The *Derby Telegraph*, 1924.'

'Any idea what evidence Arthur Grover had?'

'None, but I'd like to think that if he was prepared to talk to the press, then he had a reasonable amount of evidence to substantiate his claims. I guess Caroline would have continued the chase. Sadly, it's not something I really have the time to follow up, so unless you would like to...'

'No, sorry. I'm not even sure if it has any relevance to Caroline's death. It's quite literally old news. Although...' She spun the laptop back round. 'Can you print off a copy of this article for me?'

'Of course.'

'Do you know anything about William Bennett? Not about the murder, but about him.'

'Yes, quite a lot.' A printer in the corner hummed into life. 'He was some sort of indeterminate tradesman, but his son became a carpenter. The trade became the family business and Bennett's Carpenters is still alive and well. Now run by a Graham Bennett.' He handed Ginger the printout.

'You are a sweetheart. Thank you.'

29

*J*oyce had heard Ginger enter their suite, but she was still taken by surprise when her friend burst into her bedroom with a hand over her eyes.

'Are you decent?'

'Where have you been?'

'Are you decent?'

'What do you think I'm doing, watching television naked?'

'I'm sure it wouldn't be the first time.' Ginger was right, but Joyce wasn't going to advertise the fact. Ginger removed her hand and plonked herself on the end of the bed.

'You took your time,' Joyce retorted.

'I wanted to take a look at the mermaid, for old times' sake.'

'The what?'

'It doesn't matter. Did you have a successful morning?'

Joyce recounted her conversation with Robert Rippon Duke and concluded that no, it hadn't been particularly useful. Although he had said that Caroline seemed distracted, Joyce wasn't sure that not answering her emails as quickly as usual was a sure sign that something was wrong. Some days, Joyce couldn't be bothered replying to her emails either.

When she asked how Ginger's morning had gone, she was greeted with the smile of a child who wants to show her parent she'd got a gold star at school that day. It was actually rather endearing. Ginger pulled out a folded and rather crinkled piece of paper from her pocket and proceeded to smooth it onto the bed, trying to press out the wrinkles as she went.

'Take a look at that.'

Joyce read it quickly, but couldn't see why Ginger was looking so pleased. A second reading didn't offer any enlightenment either. Ginger tutted and prodded the paper.

'Bennett, the chap who confessed to murder, is the great-great-great – I'm not sure how many greats – something or other of Graham Bennett, the carpenter who's been working here for Dennis. He has access to all the rooms, even when they are off limits to the public. He's also bound to have met Caroline numerous times while working here. Lewis confirmed that it's the same local family-run business that William's son started.'

'Who's Lewis?'

'The very cute curator up at the museum.'

'How cute?'

'Very cute in a boyish kind of a... don't even think about it. He's young enough to be your son and... oh, never mind, just don't. He's checked and William, or rather his son, kick-started the family business which is now owned and operated by Graham Bennett.'

'So Graham's multiple great something or other murdered Caroline's great something or other?'

'Precisely.'

Joyce picked up the photocopy and read it again. 'It's one hell of a coincidence, I agree, but do you think it's a motive for murder? I can't imagine someone's reputation being damaged by a crime that happened 217 years ago.'

'Graham might not see it that way. He's built his reputation on being a local family firm – reliable, decent – and he's done very well for himself. Dennis said he is being offered more and more work, so surely he wouldn't want anything to sour that. Who knows? Perhaps Caroline told him about their ancestors' connection and he flipped in a moment of panic. Maybe he's a secret psychopath and doesn't need a motive.'

Joyce got up off the bed and grabbed Ginger by the hand.

'Come on, my little ray of sunshine. We'll ask Dennis when Graham is next due in and we'll speak to him. Right now, I'm starving and we're having lunch.'

'I've already had lunch; I grabbed a sandwich on the way back.' Joyce was put out and it must have shown in her expression because Ginger added hastily, 'I'm sure I can eat something else, though.'

'I *know* you can.'

30

*A*fter a rather enjoyable morning, Ginger was not ecstatic about the afternoon that was to follow. Seeing if they could get any information out of Lydia Foyle – yes, that she was looking forward to. Experiencing her first trip to a health spa, not so much. It was not the idea of wandering around in a towel or having someone pummel her into a state of wellbeing, which is how she described it when she was feeling charitable; it was more that she didn't know how to behave or what to do. Did she take all her clothes off or just some of them? Was she meant to talk to the masseuse, or whatever they were called, or was that not the done thing? She was pretty sure she'd end up with some slices of cucumber on her eyes and have to remember not to eat them. There was also no doubt she'd fall asleep during the massage and start to snore.

There was little that unnerved or embarrassed Ginger. She was quite proud of her bull in a china shop reputation, but spas, even just the thought of them, put her on edge. Besides which, she hadn't shaved her legs for thirty years and she was pretty sure that would be frowned upon.

Oh, stuff 'em, she thought. *If I do something inappropriate, it's not like I'll ever see them again.*

Ginger followed Joyce into the spa and was hit by a blinding white light. The room was all white walls and a white ceiling full of little white lights. A photograph of a waterfall in a rainforest filled one wall. Overall, it was spacious and meant, Ginger assumed, to create an atmosphere of calm. However, the music, if it could be called that, made Ginger want to pull her teeth out. To a backdrop of forest sounds, a pulsating pan pipe was probably in time with the average heart rate. If it was meant to make Ginger feel calm, it wasn't working. She wanted to run out the door, light a cigarette – something she hadn't done for forty years, give or take the occasional slip – and head to the nearest dark pub full of old men in flat caps who'd all stare at her when she walked in. She'd feel a sight more comfortable there than she did in here.

Joyce, on the other hand, looked very much at home.

'Good afternoon, ladies, can I be of assistance?' The young woman who addressed them had on a white uniform which would have looked like surgical scrubs, if it wasn't for the pink flowers that wound their way up the front.

'Yes, I believe you can. We have a 2pm booking.' Joyce was doing her best 'duchess' voice.

'Ms Brocklehurst? Yes, I have you here. Would you both be kind enough to take a seat while I let Lydia know you're here? She'll take you through. Can I get you anything while you wait?'

'Water please,' replied Joyce, 'with ice and lemon.'

'Certainly.'

'Water?' Ginger asked after the woman had left the room. 'For you to add some gin to?'

'I'm not going to drink it, but it keeps them in their place.'

Ginger shook her head. She picked up a menu – if that's what you called it – and looked at the list of treatments.

'Paraffin body wrap? Bloody hell, is a fire crew on standby?' Joyce raised her eyebrows higher than Ginger felt was necessary. 'Herbal body wrap? Ha, that just gives me the image of you wrapped in a rosemary bush. We could stick you in an oven with the Sunday roast.'

Joyce tutted.

'Underwater jet massage? Well, I can't do that, I didn't bring my snorkel. How about... spot treatment? I'm not sixteen; I haven't had zits for years...'

'It's not spot as in *zits*.' Joyce made the word sound like a horrific disease. 'They focus on a spot, an area of your body. Will you take this seriously?'

'How can I take it seriously when one of the things they offer is stoning? I'm sure there are some cultures in the world that would deem me worthy of such a treatment, but this is Buxton, for heaven's sake. Burning at the stake is much more de rigueur around here.'

'What are you...? Oh, hot stones, you fool, hot stones. Smooth flat stones are heated, and then placed on parts of your body. They're made out of basalt and have all sorts of benefits.'

'What, like aiding the masseuse person, therapist, whatever in emptying your wallet?'

'Shhhhh! She's coming.'

'Hello there, welcome to the Royal Spa. I'm Lydia. Now I believe that one of you is having the full Swedish massage with me?'

'That will be me.' Joyce stood. 'And I've booked my friend Ginger in for a rejuvenating facial and a pedicure.'

'Yes, Butterfly will be with you a moment.'

Ginger caught Joyce's eye and pulled a face as she mouthed *Butterfly?*

Before Lydia led her away, Joyce turned to Ginger and whispered, 'You should be grateful, I could have had you stoned.'

31

*J*oyce settled face down on the massage table and closed her eyes. She had to confess, she had taken a great deal of satisfaction from seeing Ginger's reaction to all the treatments; her friend had looked a little like a rabbit in the headlights, the poor thing. But she'd found it within herself to choose some nice, simple 'entry level' treatments for Ginger.

Lydia asked Joyce how firm she liked the pressure in her massage.

'Most definitely at the firm end of the spectrum, I'm not a delicate flower.'

'Excellent, but do please let me know if it becomes uncomfortable at any point.'

'Don't worry, I'll speak up.'

Joyce let Lydia get started and felt herself relax. Eventually, she decided it was time to dive in with as much tact as she could muster.

'It's a tragedy what happened at the weekend,' she said through the hole her face was resting in on the massage table.

'Tragedy?'

'The death at the hotel round the corner, and in somewhere as dignified as Buxton. Such a tragedy.' If she'd given Lydia reason to be concerned, the woman didn't miss a beat and the massage continued smoothly.

'Oh yes. Murder, wasn't it? Just awful.'

Good, thought Joyce, *she was first to mention murder.*

'It's a lovely hotel, I'm staying there at the moment. Have you ever been? I don't suppose you've had reason to, being local.'

No response. *Oh, to hell with it,* she thought.

'You know, now I think about it, you look rather familiar. You have stayed there, haven't you?'

There was a brief pause before Lydia spoke, a little uncertainly.

'Yes, yes, I have. It's very nice.'

'It must have been recently, I only checked in on Saturday. Just before the body was found. Were you staying then?'

Another pause.

'We… I mean, I checked out that lunchtime.'

'We? How lovely, it's the perfect place for a nice, romantic getaway. I'm sorry, I rather assumed you meant you'd stayed with a partner.'

There was something about being face down and staring at the floor, unable to see Lydia's face and her reactions, that made this a little easier. Although it also put Joyce in a position of vulnerability if Lydia got annoyed by the line of questioning. She decided not to think about that too much.

'I'm sorry, is that a sore point? I hope you're alright and I haven't touched on a sensitive subject.'

'It's alright, it's just… well, I s'pose you could say that we're in different places. We want different things.'

'Oh, I know exactly what you mean, I've been in that position many times.' Joyce was pleased Ginger wasn't in the room to make a joke about exactly what positions she had been in. 'And you went to the hotel to try and work things out, or escape the issue for a while?'

'Oh, neither, really. It's the only way we can be together and, well… something is better than nothing. I don't think things will change.' Lydia seemed to be warming up to the subject, welcoming a chance to talk, Joyce guessed.

'It's the only way you can be together?'

'Yes, I have a lodger who can't see us together because my boyfriend is… well, he's…'

'Not available?' Joyce suggested tactfully.

'No, he's not available.'

'Oh, I've been there too.' Joyce really had. 'Creeping around, grabbing snatched moments, telling myself it's better than nothing, that I'll do whatever it takes to make it work.' Joyce was momentarily surprised by how much she had said and pulled back a bit. 'Mind you, I saw a lot of nice hotels.'

She heard Lydia sigh. Joyce had hit a nerve, so she decided to steer the conversation in a different direction.

'You know, I've just thought: if you've stayed at The Lodge, you must have known Caroline, the woman who was killed, or at least seen her around.'

'Many times. She used to give talks in that costume – who was she meant to be?'

'Mary, Queen of Scots.'

'That's right. But no, I didn't know her, I just saw her around. I wanted to go on one of her tours, but John didn't like her, so we never did.'

'Why didn't John like her?' It briefly crossed Joyce's mind that this was a very expensive conversation; it had better be worth her while.

'She'd worked it out, about us. She made a couple of comments. John was furious; he would have complained, only he didn't want to draw any attention to us. It didn't bother me.'

'What did Caroline say?'

'There were a couple of pointed comments. For example, when we walked past her talking to some guests, she'd quickly turn the conversation to the mistresses of kings, or people who had come to stay at The Lodge in order to have affairs. It wasn't very subtle, but it wasn't a big deal.'

Joyce propped herself up on her elbows and turned to look at Lydia.

'How angry was John?'

'Oh, he was mad, he's got a bit of a temper. I thought he was going to have a go at her a couple of times, but I steered him away before he could say anything.'

Joyce lay back down.

'Okay, I'm ready for you to turn over.'

Joyce had had enough massages to know the routine and waited for Lydia to take hold of the towel so it didn't move as she did. Silence descended as Lydia continued the massage and Joyce thought about a man with a quick temper who had been annoyed by Caroline's comments.

32

*G*inger wondered if she'd stepped through the wardrobe into Narnia. Only she was wearing a towel robe, which was utterly unsuitable for the snow-covered world that lay beyond the coats.

'Where are we? What is this?' The walls of the small room – well, it was more of a cave – were made of rough white bricks. The ceiling was wildly uneven; it looked like a cross between white honeycomb, snow, rocks, and in places it hung down like stalactites. Below her feet was rough white sand.

'This, Ginger Salt, is a salt cave. I could hardly bring you here and not have you experience your namesake.'

'And what do we do in a salt cave? Lick the walls?' Ginger wasn't being serious, but she wouldn't be surprised if something so ridiculous was expected of her.

'Sit, relax, focus on your breathing and enjoy having your respiratory system cleansed.'

Ginger didn't believe a word and made sure her face illustrated that. Joyce let out a long sigh and sat in a wooden lounger.

'We're clearly not going to have a moment of tranquillity, let alone twenty-five minutes, so come on then: how were the treatments? I intentionally chose ones that wouldn't, or shouldn't, disturb you too much.'

Ginger frowned. She didn't like to think of herself as unadventurous, this just wasn't her kind of thing. Or did that make her unadventurous? She was no longer sure and felt a little concerned; maybe she should dive in and have a herbal-wrapped mud bath while being buried under a cairn to prove her point.

'Fine. I mean, it was a bit weird, but I suppose I found the facial relaxing. It smelt nice. I'm not sure it's necessary, though.'

'It's not about what's necessary, although personally, I think they are if you want to look after yourself. It's about enjoyment, relaxation, rejuvenation...'

'Expenditure, laziness...'

Joyce looked annoyed by Ginger's additions to the list. Ginger was only complaining to wind her friend up, plus she hadn't been prepared to like it. Joyce was right, and that was irritating to say the least.

'Alright, yes, it was okay and I might even consider having another. And you can take that smirk off your face; you were right about the facial, but not the bloody pedicure. It was ticklish, I hate people touching my feet. They're fine as they are.'

'I've seen your feet, and I sometimes wonder if you need a blacksmith to come and shoe them.'

Ginger couldn't help but laugh at that; Joyce wasn't far off. The pedicure hadn't been a huge success, she'd giggled through most of it and kept pulling her feet away, but they did feel like they'd had a good scrub.

They settled down on the wooden loungers, their legs out in front of them, closed their eyes and took a deep breath. That was it, as long as Ginger could manage.

'Come on, then, what did she say?'

'I'd hoped that could wait until we were back at the hotel.'

'Not a chance, this is murder we're talking about. Spit it out, woman.'

Joyce filled in Ginger, who then responded by letting out a long whistle.

'Well, well, well. We have a man with a lot to lose and Caroline has rubbed him up the wrong way. Shame she couldn't keep her opinions to herself, she might still be alive.'

'We can't jump to the conclusion that it's him.'

'I don't know. Her constant digs could have pushed him into a place of uncontrollable rage and he planned to kill her on his next stay. He made direct contact with her and asked for a talk or tour of some kind, and then he killed her when she arrived.'

Joyce looked doubtful. 'If she disapproved of his and Lydia's relationship, then I can't imagine she'd be keen to give them a tour. Her morals – if they were that strongly held – probably wouldn't allow it.'

'He's not going to have used his own name, is he? And he could disguise his voice. Especially if he was concerned that she might mention to someone that she was going to meet him; that would have had the police onto him in no time at all after the murder.'

'Okay,' Joyce said as she settled back into her lounger, her eyes closed. 'Add him to the list. I want to get my money's worth before we head back.'

*A*fter being scrubbed, smoothed and pummelled, and then sweating inside an enormous salt cellar, Joyce and Ginger had walked slowly back to the hotel in the slightly dazed state that comes from having other people pamper your body while you gaze introspectively. This trip to Buxton might not have gone in the direction that Joyce was expecting, but she couldn't describe it as unpleasant; in fact, she was rather enjoying it.

She finished putting on her makeup, listening to the sound of Ginger bustling away in the room next door, and smiled. Joyce had never had many 'girlfriends': other women to go shopping or have a weekend away with. It was only recently that she had started to develop some close friendships at work. Previously, she had always been running around after one husband or another, busy at work, or just too independent to feel that she needed a confidante. She'd had lots of pals, plenty of people who were up for a trip to the theatre or out for dinner, but she doubted she'd call on any of them if she was in the midst of a crisis. It was comforting to know that was changing, although Joyce couldn't imagine a situation that she couldn't cope with on her own.

There was a crash, followed by, 'Oh bugger, you idiot.' Joyce smiled again; she was relishing her time with Ginger. Her friend wasn't the most graceful of people and she could swear like a sailor – although, so could Joyce given the right circumstances. But Ginger was funny and kind, and gutsy. Joyce liked gutsy women; anything less than that and Joyce would lose patience.

There was another crash.

'What the heck? Ginger, are you alright?'

'Yes, yes, fine,' came the response from the open door on the far side of the sitting room. 'Quite alright, see you in the bar.'

Ginger closed the door and Joyce shook her head. Was it the coffee table? A lamp? She started mentally listing all the delicate objects she might have to consider tucking away in her own home the next time Ginger came round.

The bar was quiet when Joyce arrived. Lisa, the bar manager, was chatting to a customer as Joyce pulled herself gracefully onto a stool. She made sure the split in her skirt revealed a little thigh and long legs which led to a pair of scarlet shoes, then spun the seat round so she was facing the bar.

Joyce always felt particularly good after a visit to a spa. She would normally schedule them for a Saturday so she could head out that evening, show off her glowing skin and relax even further into a bottle of champagne. The fact that it was actually a Monday wouldn't stop her, especially when her weekend break had turned into a week off work; she was going to make the most of it, murder or no murder.

Dennis gave a low whistle as he walked past her with his hands full of delicately balanced wine glasses. He came to a stop, stared at the door, and gave a second whistle with a little more oomph this time.

'Lady Salt, you look particularly delightful this evening.'

Ginger stood in the doorway pulling a dramatic catwalk pose, one hand reaching for the top of the door frame, the other on her hip. She was wearing a loose-fitting burnt orange silk suit which flowed over her voluminous curves. With an exaggerated sashay, she walked to the stool next to Joyce and, with a little less grace than her friend, hoisted herself up.

'Who are you and what've you done with Ginger?' Joyce asked with an arched eyebrow.

'Give over, you've seen me all gussied up before.'

'Not on a Monday. You should go to a spa more often.'

'I have to admit, and I hate to say this, but I do feel rather good. I just decided that I would show off this afternoon's efforts.'

Joyce gave her another once-over. 'Nice suit.'

'Cheers, I made it.'

Joyce's eyes nearly popped out. 'You really do know your way around the sewing machine.'

'Did you think I was lying when I said I was a seamstress?' Ginger shook her head. 'Ye of little faith. Yes, I do know what I'm doing and, if you play your cards right, I'll whip one up for you.'

'I'll hold you to that.' Joyce took a final look, admiring the silver ringlets that Ginger had curled her hair into. The silver had a noticeable shine to it.

'Is it someone's birthday?' Dennis asked as he placed two coasters in front of them. 'Or are you on the pull?'

'What are you saying?' Ginger asked with a glint in her eye. 'That the rest of the time I'm a scruffy old bag lady?'

'Would I dare?'

'No, but you'd dare think it.'

'Well, I have never thought such a thing. Can I pour you a drink? That way, it will look less like a set-up when Graham gets here.' Ginger and Joyce had shared their findings with Dennis earlier. It turned out Graham was due to drop by this evening to give Dennis an invoice.

'Crack open the bubbles, please, barman,' instructed Joyce. 'The good stuff.'

'You know, I might have to get you to cover the bar bill at this rate.' Joyce had forgotten that the bonus of their free week in the hotel was less of a bonus for Dennis, who was at risk of having his bar profits drained.

'Tell you what, if we solve this before Friday, in time for your little shindig, you cover the tab. If we don't, we'll pay.'

He considered Joyce's proposal. 'It's a deal.'

'Hang on a minute,' Ginger didn't look quite so happy with it, 'maybe we should open a different bottle if those are the rules, just to be on the safe side.'

'To hell with that. Dennis, don't you dare place a substandard bottle of champagne before me.'

'How dare you suggest I'd stock anything substandard.'

'Fair enough. Cheers!' Joyce took the glass from his hand as soon as Dennis finished pouring the champagne.

He laughed. 'Thirsty much?'

Joyce raised the glass at him before taking a drink.

'You two look very much at home here. Have you ever thought of retiring and becoming mystery visitors? You could spend your golden years in the world's finest hotels, experiencing every aspect of their services and not having to spend a penny. I can't imagine anything would pass you two by. Hotel staff the world over would be terrified of a visit by the famous Joyce and Ginger. You'd have to start wearing disguises and have an endless supply of pseudonyms.'

Joyce was about to answer when she spotted someone walk into the bar. She had no idea who he was, but she *wanted* to know.

34

Ginger saw the expression on Joyce's face and turned to see what she was looking at. It was no surprise that 'what' was actually a 'who', and a good-looking male one at that. He had the rugged, healthy look of someone who did at least some of his work outside and was rather fit as a result.

'Dennis,' the newcomer strode up to the bar and shook hands with the hotel owner, 'how's it going?'

'Very well, thank you, Graham. Can I get you a drink?'

'You certainly can, and here's a little something for you.' The man handed over an envelope. 'Sorry it's not as nice as a drink.'

Dennis laughed. 'Not a problem, I'll make sure you're paid by the end of the week. Can I introduce you to a couple of friends of mine? This is Ginger, and this is Joyce. Ladies, this is the best carpenter around, Graham Bennett.'

'Nice to meet you, ladies.' Graham didn't take a seat, instead opting to stand at the end of the bar close to Dennis.

'Nice car.' Dennis was looking out of the window at a shiny Mercedes convertible. 'That'll be fun in the summer when you can take the top down.'

'Yeah, thought I'd treat myself.'

'Graham is always in demand,' Dennis explained to Ginger and Joyce, 'not surprisingly.'

'I've been lucky.'

'Pah, no luck involved. I wouldn't have anyone else touch my place; it's you and your team or no one.'

'You've been working on the rooms upstairs?' Ginger asked. Graham replied with a nod as he took a drink of beer and wiped his top lip clean of froth. 'I only saw one briefly, but it looked lovely.'

'These two had a bit of a shock. They found Caroline's body on Saturday morning.'

Graham screwed his face up. 'Bloody awful what happened, that must have been a nightmare for you both. Can't imagine you've slept well after that.'

'We're coming to terms with it. Actually, we've both found that learning more about Caroline – being able to imagine her as a real flesh-and-blood person – helps us cope. Doesn't it, Joyce?'

'It does.' Joyce didn't move her eyes from the man in front of her, and Ginger was of the impression that Graham knew exactly the effect he was having on her.

'So, we've been speaking to people about her research.' Graham locked eyes with Ginger, but there was no malice there, just curiosity. 'Her family had a very close link to Buxton; it's been fascinating to read about it.' Graham just nodded and took another drink. 'Did you have the chance to get to know her? You must have seen her a lot.'

He put his glass down. 'I did. She was interesting, had a lot to say once she got going, which wasn't always a good thing. But she was alright, was Caroline, and it's a tragedy what happened. We talked about the history of this place; she'd been doing research on some of the old guests, hadn't she, Dennis? She'd often tell me about it when I took a tea break.'

'We found a reference to a Bennett who was a carpenter when we were looking at her family history.' Joyce had lost her glazed look. 'That wouldn't be your ancestor, would it?' For a woman as feisty as she, Joyce had perfected the *ever so sweetly curious* look that was planted firmly on her face.

'It would indeed.'

'Oh then... oh my! Well, does that mean that one of your family... well he... did he...?'

Ginger had to stop herself laughing at Joyce's impression of horrified lady.

'It does indeed. I'm afraid that Caroline and I had a rather unfortunate connection. My ancestor murdered her ancestor.' He said it so casually that Ginger felt mildly uncomfortable, but then, it had happened a very long time ago.

'That must have come as quite a shock. Did you have any idea before Caroline mentioned it?' Dennis asked.

'Not a clue. My father didn't say anything, but then the only thing we really talked about was the work. I could be a direct descendant of William the Conqueror and I wouldn't have a clue because no one would've said anything.'

'It was probably something your father – and you – would rather people didn't find out about,' said Ginger.

'Why? It happened over 200 years ago, it's nothing to do with me. In fact, Caroline and I were talking about making it public knowledge. She said it would make her tours more personal and I reckon she was right. People love to hear about stuff like that, and to have a direct descendant stood in front of them, telling the story; I reckon she'd have been raking it in. It also wouldn't have done me any harm, it would have made a great story about how, two centuries later, the descendants of victim and murderer had got to know each other and there was no hard feelings. Instead, they were telling the story as a sort of reconciliation. There'd be articles in the papers, free advertising for me.'

Ginger, who wasn't distracted by his looks, felt it all sounded a little too easy, too rehearsed. She was sure that Caroline would have wanted to build the story into her tours, but she didn't think she'd be very interested in appearing in newspapers or *raking it in.* This was a woman who was happy to work as a cleaner in a hotel where she had the flexibility to pursue her true passion. After she'd been a couple of years back in Buxton, it wasn't unreasonable to imagine Caroline finding better-paid work, or she could have sold the family house and bought a cheaper flat, leaving money for her to spend on other things, but Ginger wasn't convinced. She wondered if Graham assumed it would be easy to turn on the charm and pull the wool over the eyes of a couple of women. It wasn't going to work on her. Joyce, on the other hand... well, she looked smitten. Ginger just hoped that too was an act.

'So, when you going on a date?' The two women had moved to their sitting room.

'What on earth are you talking about?'

Ginger laughed at Joyce's feigned innocence. 'You do a very convincing fawning act, you must have men the world over sure that you have never seen anyone so handsome, that there is nothing you wouldn't do for them. It's amazing how you can turn that on. From hard as nails one minute to pretend putty in their hands the next.'

'It's true, I have left a trail of broken hearts, although that's mainly because I ripped them out with my bare hands when they got a bit too keen.'

'And ate them with a nice chianti?'

'Never! A shiraz perhaps. So, what do you think about our handsome carpenter?' Joyce settled herself onto the sofa as she waited for Ginger's response.

'Bit full of himself, but I know that's not what you meant. I'm not sure; I agree that a 200-year-old murder is an unlikely motive, so he's not at the top of my list, but there was something about him that left me uneasy. I'm not sure the "reconciliation" is as simple as he tried to make it sound. If anything, he tried too hard, which makes me think he's up to something. I just don't know what.'

'Okay, so we put him on the back burner for now. What's next?'

'After what Lydia told you, I think we go and talk to John Bradbury. I know Dennis is worried, but I'm sure we can keep him, and the hotel, out of this.'

'Excellent. Well, it's time for my beauty sleep.' Ginger glanced at her watch. 'Don't you dare, Ginger Salt! I know what you're going to say, and no, I should not have gone to bed hours ago. See you in the morning. You're in charge of coffee and you can bring it to me in bed.'

'What did your last slave… oh, forget it. Goodnight.'

35

*G*inger pulled the car onto a wet, sandy piece of land, and she and Joyce sat and stared through the chain-link fence at the half-built street of houses. They'd called by the offices of Peak District Plumbers in the hope of being able to talk to John Bradbury, but the receptionist had told them he was out on a job, which had led them to the outskirts of Buxton.

Some basic research had told them that John had started out as a plumber almost twenty years ago and was now one of the most successful self-made businessmen in the area. He was reported to be worth a few million pounds. Not only did he run a plumbing empire, but he had branched out into building houses. In front of them was a small development of only six homes, each of which was being built in an array of bespoke styles to avoid the 'estate' feel. Looking at them, however, Joyce couldn't see anything that distinguished them from any other new-build project she'd seen.

The sun had finally deigned to show its face, and Joyce could think of plenty of places she would rather be than a building site, but needs must.

'Come on, then, let's get this over with.' She reached for the door handle, but Ginger stopped her.

'Hang on, if he wants to know why we've driven here just to ask him about Caroline, what do we say?'

'We're relatives and we want to find out what happened to our beloved niece.'

'And if Lydia told him about us?'

'That's not a problem. She never asked me who I was or why I was interested, so it's not as though I've told her something different.'

Ginger seemed happy with that idea and they stepped out into the cold air.

'Ha, well, you're going to make someone's day.' Ginger indicated towards a van with *Bennett's Family Carpenters* on the side.

'Not so great if he gives the game away. Hopefully he'll be working in a different house, away from John.'

Ginger grunted an agreement as she pulled the collar up on her coat and made a tentative approach towards the gate. She had on her sensible walking shoes, but she didn't fancy getting wet feet again. Joyce strode past her.

'You're practically wearing flippers, pick up the pace.'

They had barely reached the gate when Joyce grabbed Ginger by the sleeve of her coat and pulled her behind a skip over-flowing with rocks and scraps of wood.

'Hey, what the heck? Alright, you can let go now. What is it?'

They peeped over the top. Joyce had spotted both John Brad-bury and Graham Bennett. They were standing outside a Portak-abin that looked as if it was being used as an office. John was holding a mug, but it was being waved about in all directions and Joyce doubted it still held any liquid. He looked to be in control of the proceedings, though. Graham, on the other hand, stood with his hands in his pockets; he looked defiant, but didn't say anything.

'Can you hear what they're sayin'?' Ginger whispered. Joyce

shook her head. The two men continued in this way for a couple of minutes before Graham made what was clearly some kind of parting comment, and then stormed off towards one of the houses. Whatever had been said, it hadn't gone his way.

'Come on.' Joyce grabbed Ginger's sleeve again and pulled her out into the open.

'Get off! He looks happy enough, but we still need to tread carefully. If what Lydia said is true, then he has one hell of a temper.'

Joyce agreed, but didn't say anything. She was a little nervous, despite the effect she generally had on men. Uncharacteristically tentatively, she knocked on the door.

'WHAT?'

After a quick glance at Ginger, Joyce led the way in. John looked genuinely taken aback.

'What are you doing here? I mean, hello.' He stood; a gentleman was hiding somewhere behind the gruff exterior.

'John Bradbury?' Joyce took the lead.

'Yes.'

'I'm Joyce and this is my sister, Ginger.' If that had been true, then he couldn't have been blamed for thinking that one of them had been the result of a liaison with the postman or milkman.

'How can I help? I'm afraid if you're interested in one of the houses, they've all been sold.'

'No, no, it's not that. Oh, this is so difficult and I don't really know where to start.' Joyce looked round at Ginger as though seeking support. 'It's just that we're trying to get some information about a rather dreadful incident and we think you might be able to help.'

John grabbed a couple of seats and put them in front of his desk.

'I've no idea how I can be of assistance, but fire away, ladies. What's this all about?' His skin had the orange hue of someone who was a little too fond of tanning beds, but if you looked beyond that, he was good-looking with strong features and blue eyes. His voice was gruff, but capable of a kindly tone.

'Well, I think that you might have been staying at The Lodge in Buxton on the night of the 19th.'

'How do you know that?'

Joyce could see his expression harden, but she'd been expecting it.

'Oh, just someone who recognised you saw you in passing. Said you were there on your own and might have seen something.'

'And what am I meant to have seen?'

'Someone died in tragic circumstances on the Saturday morning and we wondered if you saw something out of the ordinary?' Joyce was keeping her voice soft and low. She played with a handkerchief she had taken out of her pocket.

'Can't say I did. Why you asking questions anyway? The police have already been here to talk to me.'

'The victim was our niece.'

'A dear friend.'

The two responses collided and Ginger rectified her error.

'Niece, she was our niece.' She cringed, simultaneously mouthing *sorry* at Joyce as John briefly glanced away.

'And we just want to know what happened. The police will do a fine job, I'm sure, but they're bound to be slowed down by rules and regulations, and we don't want to wait. We just want to be able to move on. The whole family does.' Joyce dropped her eyes briefly, and then dabbed at the corners with her handkerchief.

'Right. Well, like I said to the police, I didn't know her and didn't see anything.'

'Do you stay there often? It seems like the ideal place to stay if you've had a late night at work, that would be a very sensible thing to do.'

'I do stay there quite a bit, I often work late.'

'So you must have seen her – Caroline – around the hotel quite a lot.'

'From time to time. She did my room a few times and I saw her talking to people about history.'

'Do you have an interest in history?'

'A little.'

'Did you ever listen when she was giving history talks to other guests?'

'Why would I want to?'

Joyce took a deep breath. He was going to keep insisting he knew nothing, unless she pushed him.

'I believe they were very interesting: local history, famous visitors, kings and queens, their *mistresses*.' She smiled, trying to play it cool, spotting the colour starting to rise in his cheeks. She felt Ginger's foot nudge against hers.

I know what I'm doing, Joyce thought, but was pleased they were on the opposite side of the desk to John and next to the door.

'What ya getting at? Has someone at the hotel been saying something? They should mind their own damned business! I pay good money and I expect some privacy in return.'

'Oh absolutely, and the hotel has not told us anything. They've refused to answer any of our questions.'

'I should hope so.'

That was it. Joyce was tired of pussyfooting around.

'Mr Bradshaw, did you and Caroline ever have an argument?'

'What the hell are you getting at?' He stood quickly and his chair fell over. 'Who did you say you were?'

'We're just…'

'Family? Rubbish! I don't believe it. Tell me what you want, and then get the hell out of here.'

'Alright, Mr Bradshaw.' Joyce stood; she matched his height inch for inch. 'We've been told that Caroline said something that made you very angry – angry enough to lose your temper, perhaps?'

'Who told you? That's utter rubbish! We might have exchanged a few words – she didn't know how to mind her own business – but that was ages ago and I never touched her. That's not my style. I'd never hit a woman.'

'A man?'

'Maybe, if he deserved it.'

'What were you and Graham Bennett talking about?'

His face took on a different expression. Not just anger, it had gone up a notch. He looked like a man who was about to lose control.

'GET OUT. NOW!'

Joyce dropped her act; it was time to do as he said. She stared wide eyed at Ginger, who turned and shot out of the door, narrowly avoiding falling down the steps. They both walked away as quickly as they could.

'Well, he's definitely got a temper,' Ginger panted as they half ran back to her car. 'He's got it in him to flip.'

'I don't know, I believe him when he says he wouldn't hit a woman. Bit different with the blokes; I wouldn't be surprised if he'd threaten someone who crossed him. Not sure he'd hit them, though. He's all talk and no trousers.'

They'd reached the car and Ginger got her keys out as she spoke. 'And he might not be doing as well as people think. There was a solicitor's letter on his desk. It could just be standard business, but it might also be bad news.'

'I saw that. I recognise the firm: it's from a solicitor who specialises in divorce.'

'Then of course you'd recognise it, you've probably kept the company afloat.'

The door to the Portakabin was flung open and John Bradbury scanned the carpark until his eyes landed on their car.

'Christ, Ginger, get in and put your foot down.'

36

*G*inger set off at a fair pace. If truth be told, she had been rather energised by throwing the car into gear and speeding off as if she was in an episode of *The Sweeney*, her favourite police drama back in the 1970s. It was a very long time since she had felt that sort of adrenalin, whether it was from fleeing an orchard as a child with her skirts full of apples after a morning's scrumping, or snatched kisses with a lover. She needed a bit more excitement in her life.

The thought of running, chasing and climbing gave her an idea. She glanced over at Joyce, whose outfit was a cross between Miss Marple and Katherine Hepburn with a little Gina Lollobrigida thrown in for good measure. Joyce's tweed jacket was tight enough to ensure that some of her finest assets popped out like little Chihuahuas wanting to admire the view. Her tight brown trousers were so closely fitting, they left little to the imagination, but then Joyce's legs were worthy of the attention.

'So, where next, driver? Is it time for lunch yet?'

Ginger glanced at the dashboard. The clock was one of the few things working on it, her speed a permanent guessing game.

'Hardly, it's just turned eleven. We still have time for another little adventure.'

Joyce looked doubtful and Ginger tossed her a bag of mints. At least with one of those in her mouth, she might be less likely to complain.

Ginger turned off the main road and into a street mainly consisting of bungalows, then onto a road of large stone family houses. It wasn't at all obvious where they were going until, after following a street of more large houses with mature trees and tall well-kept hedges, Ginger turned into a carpark with a large sign for 'Treetops'.

'Good idea,' declared Joyce as she examined the sign. 'We can talk to Ed in the café.'

'I'm not sure it will meet your exacting standards, but we can probably get a cup of builders' tea and a flapjack.' A bucket of tea strong enough to make hairs grow on your chest sounded like just the ticket right now, and Ginger was partial to a flapjack. She liked them tough enough that you could use them to build a garden wall, but with the right of amount of internal chewiness that they got stuck to your teeth and provided a continuous source of snack throughout the day.

They walked into a large Swiss chalet-style building and stopped at the ticket desk. A young man was scrolling through his phone.

'Two adults?' he asked, barely glancing up.

'We just want to talk to Ed Weeks. I believe he works here?'

'Yep, head through there. They'll be able to tell you where he is.' He pointed, but still didn't look up. They followed his directions out of the back door and towards another smaller wooden chalet. Beyond was a thick forest, the screams and laughter of children bursting from within the branches.

A group of teenagers with a handful of adults came trailing along a path towards them, grinning and giggling, playfully pushing and shoving.

'*Did you see...?*

'*I can't believe I did that...*'

'*It was so frightening...*'

'*It was hilarious when you...*'

Ginger smiled at their joie de vivre. She wished school trips had involved this sort of thing in her day. She wished they'd *had* school trips in her day.

As they entered the chalet, another young man greeted them. Ginger could have sworn she saw him smirk as he gave them the once-over.

'We'd like to have a chat with Ed Weeks.'

'He's up on the zip line, but he's just had his break so he won't be back for a while.'

'There's no way we can have just five minutes of his time?'

He looked at Ginger like she was out of her mind.

'Health and safety, he can't leave his post. You could go see him, though.' He grinned, not entirely with kindness, and waved his hand towards a wall of harnesses.

'Alright, we will.' His face fell and he just stared at Ginger. Joyce grabbed her shoulder.

'Are you out of your mind? I'm not going up there.'

'It'll be fun, won't it...' Ginger peered at the lad's badge, '... Ric?' She watched as Joyce registered the look of disbelief on Ric's face, then took a deep breath. Joyce hated to be underestimated as much as she did.

'Agreed. I think that green harness will go nicely with my outfit.'

'That's not how we decide...' Ric took the harness off the wall. 'Actually, that will probably work.' He took a red one for Ginger. 'That colour okay?' His words dripped with sarcasm.

'Perfect. Now, get on with it.'

Ric, incredulity solidly etched on his face, helped the two women into the harnesses. He would look up at them from time to time as though he expected them to laugh and tell him it was all a joke, but Ginger was dead set and starting to look forward to it. Joyce stumbled a little as Ric pulled the waist belt tight.

'Careful, I'm out of practice. It's some time since I've had a man get me into a harness.' She gave him a look of comical seduction and his expression changed to one of panic.

'Be nice,' Ginger advised her. 'Our lives are in his hands.'

'So is my pleasure,' Joyce added.

'You're cruel.'

'Not at all. You love it, don't you, Ric?'

Ric had lost every ounce of arrogance and become a quiet, terrified boy. He took a map from the counter top and, without looking either of them in the eye, circled a location with a marker pen.

'Follow the footpath to here. You'll bypass much of the treetop trail, and then you'll only have a couple of rope challenges to complete before you get to Ed at the zip wire. Look for a girl with blonde hair in a red t-shirt; I'll radio her to look out for you and she'll make sure you get clipped in safely.'

The young woman in the red t-shirt was indeed looking out for them.

'Well, you ain't hard to spot. Good on ya. Come on.' She attached them both to a safety line before they made their way up a wood and rope ladder attached to a tree. Ginger felt a freedom she hadn't experienced for a long time as she climbed, slowly but surely. At the top, she turned to watch Joyce. Her shoes were utterly ridiculous for what they were doing: moss-green wedge heels which added three inches to her height. There was a look of deep concentration on her face, but she made it to the top without so much as breaking a nail.

'And to think I reckoned a trip to a local hotel was going to be boring. You are buying me a very strong drink when we get back.'

Joyce momentarily lost her grip and flailed, hovering backwards over the way she had just come, before thrusting her arm out and grabbing a rope to steady herself.

'Let's get this over with.'

37

The young woman had told them the bridges and crossings were only twenty feet above the ground, but they felt at least twice that to Joyce. It wasn't that she was afraid of heights, she just preferred not to be at height on a rickety-looking rope bridge slung between two trees.

Ahead of her lay a route that would take her over a series of foot-wide wooden discs, each acting as a step towards the next one. They hung independently of one another, and Joyce watched as Ginger made her way across them, holding on to a rope tied between the same two trees for support. The discs swayed from side to side and sometimes back and forth. Ginger wobbled and lurched, one leg going one way, another the other, her free arm spinning like a windmill, her vocabulary getting more unrepeatable as she went. It was a very long time since Joyce had done the splits; she hoped she hadn't lost the flexibility.

She held on to her safety rope and gingerly stepped out. Taking her time, she gained some balance before stepping to the next one, waiting for each disc to stop swaying before moving on. She tried to think of it as a dance, but it was still unnerving and she attempted to block out how high above the ground she was.

One leg suddenly shot from under her and she screamed in a high pitch that echoed around the forest. She tried not to fight it and brought the disc back under control, silently cursing Caroline.

I don't even blooming well know you. Why did you have to get yourself killed? I hope whatever it was, was worth it.

As she progressed further along, having found a rhythm, Joyce's thoughts shifted. *After this, we better get some answers. What were you up to, girl? Help me find out so I can get off this damned thing... This isn't so bad, though; I can do this. Slow and steady...'*

She stepped with a firm and confident footing onto a ledge attached to a tree and leaned into Ginger's outstretched arms.

'You did it, old girl! You bloody did it!'

'Of course I did.' Joyce's sharp response hid a pride she felt swelling throughout her. She fancied more of this. She could see Ed up ahead at the top of a zip line and was actually pleased there were two more crossings before they got there.

'I'll lead.' Joyce gave Ginger a nod before putting a foot onto a single rope that stretched from where they were standing to the next tree. Once again, a rope on either side formed loose rails for them to hold on to. Joyce struggled to get her footing; her shoes had coped fine when she stepped onto a solid surface, but a tightrope? That was another matter.

'Oh, bugger it!' She grabbed a shoe and tossed it towards the ground, the second following close behind. Her mother had been a dancer and Joyce had attended lessons throughout her youth; familiar muscles kicked into action and she delicately stepped her away across, landing on the next platform to a round of applause from Ginger.

Joyce watched as her friend swung, dipped, cursed, screamed, laughing as Ginger clung on for dear life before landing beside her with a thud.

'Brilliant! Blooming brilliant! We're coming back here another day and doing it all.'

Joyce joined in with the laughter, looking at the new friend in her life. My God, was this woman fun.

'Ready?' Joyce asked, before disappearing along a row of narrow wooden boards which had been formed into a series of crosses. Joyce was able to step into the centre of each cross and gain the greatest amount of stability in the process. She had completely forgotten that Ed was waiting on the platform ahead and stepped calmly off the last cross and into a space beside him. His mouth was open and his eyes wide.

'Oh sorry, didn't see you there. Hang on a minute.' She turned and cheered on Ginger, who was all over the place and giggling as she wobbled from side to side.

'I don't have the knack like you. Whoa! Nearly lost it then.' Ginger cackled, and then focused. 'Look out, I'm coming.' She practically ran, looking like a drunk rag doll, and careered forwards, barrelling into Ed and knocking the wind out of him. 'Blooming brilliant!'

The two women caught their breath and straightened out their clothing.

'You're mad, completely mad,' said Ed. 'You're good, though. You must really want to talk to me.'

'We certainly do, young man, and bearing in mind what we've just put ourselves through, the least you can do is tell us the truth. Every jot of it.' Joyce was the kind of woman few dared to cross, and after what he had just seen her achieve, she doubted that Ed would attempt to buck that trend.

Once the two women had caught their breath and reminded themselves of the purpose of the visit, they looked at Ed with much more serious expressions.

'We want to hear everything you know about the thefts at The Lodge,' Joyce told him.

'I can't tell you anything. I don't know a thing.'

'You didn't get that working here,' Joyce pointed at his watch, 'or at The Lodge. I've never even dated a man who wears one of those, and I have expensive taste.'

'It was a gift, I turned eighteen a bit ago.'

'Oh well, that explains it. Makes perfect sense, if you're the son of a Russian oligarch. Who gave it to you?'

He glanced between them, looking like he needed help.

'Mum… Mum got it for me. She'd been saving for ages. She spent a ton on my sister for her twenty-first and I think she felt a bit guilty, and we're dead close as well. I was amazed 'n' all, I knew it was expensive.'

He sounded desperate. Joyce gave Ginger an almost imperceptible nod. She believed him.

'Have you any idea who has been stealing from the rooms?'

He shook his head, a little too quickly.

'Come on, you must know most things that are going on, see things, hear things.'

'No, nothin'. I swear.'

'Not even an idea? No clue?'

'No. Honest, I've no idea.'

This time, Joyce didn't believe him. There were all the usual signs: he'd stopped looking at them in the eye; he couldn't stand still. He was definitely on edge, but more than that, he was worried. Really worried. Joyce actually felt sorry for him. He was working two jobs and going to college. He wasn't a bad lad, but something was bothering him and he wasn't going to tell them what it was anytime soon.

'Alright, Ed. We'll leave that. But what can you tell us about Caroline? Was there anyone she spent a lot of time talking to? Were there any of the guests that she didn't get on with? Anything at all that was out of the ordinary?'

He seemed to think hard, but eventually shook his head.

'She was always on the go. If she wasn't cleaning rooms, she was answering questions. She made a real effort to talk to guests who were regulars. She wasn't a natural, like; a bit stiff if you ask me, but she tried. She was dead clever. She could tell you loads about the Queen. Mary. She liked talking about art and I once heard her telling some visitors about the buildings near the hotel. I learnt loads from her, but I'd just listen. We didn't speak to each other much.'

That made sense. He was a gangly teenager who was still awkward.

Ginger rested a hand against the giant tree trunk, using it to steady herself as she stepped closer to Ed.

'Was there anyone who didn't like her?

'She was always businesslike, polite, so I don't see why anyone wouldn't like her. Some just... well, ignored her, I suppose. But maybe...'

'Come on, Ed, spit it out.' Ginger smiled.

'That couple. The bloke runs his own business. We know the two of them aren't married. I did once see him and Caroline talking. He didn't look happy – not angry, just like he was frustrated. Told Caroline he'd talk to her later, and then walked off. That's it, nothing else.'

The squeals of children could be heard coming up behind them through the trees.

'I think it's time we went. How do we get down from here?' Joyce glanced around, unable to see any rope ladders. Ed grinned, but kindly.

'You'll have to go down here.' He pointed to a metal cable that was secured above their heads and stretched off through the trees. Beyond the platform they were standing on, the ground fell away. Silence descended on the trio as the women stared off into the distance.

'You sure there's no ladder?' asked Joyce quietly.

'Yeah, I'm sure. Go on, you'll love it.' He reached for a piece of equipment hanging from the cable. 'Who's first?'

Neither looked at the other. Joyce briefly considered what she'd eaten for breakfast. She wasn't keen to be reunited with it.

'Oh, for heaven's sake, let's get this over with. So long as I don't break a nail.'

'A leg maybe?' wondered Ginger out loud. Ed laughed before quickly clipping Joyce's harness onto the cable.

'On the count of three... two...' He gave Joyce a gentle shove off the platform. She felt a lurch, her stomach shooting towards her mouth as she flew off the edge. She glanced at her stockinged feet.

Dammit, I'll never get my shoes back now.

38

Ginger would never forget the way Joyce looked when she joined her at the bottom of the zip line. Her hair resembled candy floss that had got caught in a strong wind. She had mud up the back of her trousers from an indelicate landing. Ginger knew that from experience: she'd slid the final few yards on her bottom. They stared at one another, and then burst into laughter.

'We need to fetch your shoes.'

'Forget it. We're closer to the carpark than the top of that hill and it's not like I haven't got more.' Joyce took her arm as they walked along a path of wood chips.

'What did you make of him, then?' Ginger asked. 'Do you think he's telling the truth?'

'I do. I think he's a good lad, but there is something that's bothering him. It's enough for him to clam up, which means it's close to home and he's worried about dropping someone in it. I doubt he's going to tell us what it is, though. We've got as much as we can from him.'

Ginger nodded; she'd come to the same conclusion. She was surprised to hear Joyce talk about Ed with such understanding, though; it wouldn't have been a shock to see Joyce grab him, hold him over the edge of the platform and threaten to drop him. She was clearly still getting to know her new friend.

After returning to the hotel, they entered via a back door and sneaked along the corridor to their room. Joyce was determined that no one was going to see her in her present state, so the two women changed quickly and tidied themselves up. Next on their agenda was lunch and a chance to go over Caroline's notes again. Mark had copied those he felt contained the most useful information, something that was no doubt illegal and likely to get them in a lot of trouble if DS Harnby ever found out. Ginger brought a couple of magazines from their room so that the notes could quickly be hidden in them on the off chance that Harnby made an appearance.

'I think I would have liked to go on one of her tours,' said Ginger as they tucked in to lunch. 'I've lived in Derbyshire my entire life, but there's bound to be plenty I don't know.'

'Hmm.' Joyce clearly wasn't listening. Her nose was deep in the notes as she slowly consumed a salmon and cream cheese sandwich.

'You lived anywhere else?' Ginger asked.

'Hmm. What?'

'You lived anywhere else, or always been round here?'

'When I was little, my mother and I moved around quite a lot, but she decided to put down some roots here as I got older. Since then, I've had flirtations with relocations. Nowhere stuck, though, and I've always found myself back here. Listen to this: there's a mention of quite a few places around Buxton, all linked with her tours, but Morton Hall has its own set of notes. You heard of it?'

'It rings a bell, but I've no idea where it is.'

Joyce took a final bite of her sandwich before moving the plate and spreading a couple of pieces of paper out in front of her. She nursed a cup of coffee as she spoke.

'It looks like it's been everything from a large home to a hotel and a military hospital during the First World War. Caroline's notes focus on the value of some of the architectural detail, how it's essential that it be restored and remain on display and accessible to the public, or those who use the building on a regular basis. Are you sure you don't know where it is?'

'No, but I know who might. Dennis...'

He was walking past, having finished talking to a couple of hotel guests. As ever, he was resplendent in a navy blue suit. Today's tie was a purple affair with pink spots.

'Yes, madam, can I be of assistance?' he joked. Ginger briefly described the building based on Caroline's notes.

'Any idea where it is?'

'Of course, it's on the Manchester Road, heading out of town. Caroline was quite interested in it. It's for sale, but there's been a bit of controversy around it. She went to a couple of open forum meetings about it. Usual thing: some faceless construction company has got plans and wads of cash, and locals have other ideas. I don't know the details, though. Nice place. It would make a great hotel.'

'Would you be interested in buying it?'

'Heavens no, this place takes enough work. My ambitions lie here, I have no interest in establishing an empire. Even a small Buxton-based one.'

'What do you think Caroline's interest would be?' Ginger asked. 'She wasn't likely to be in a position to buy it, was she?'

'Not likely, I didn't pay her that much. If there's anything in its history worth mentioning in her tours, then I guess she'd be looking at that, but I know she also wanted to see it preserved and spent a lot of time digging up information that might help the case for that. I gave her the afternoon off one day to attend one of those meetings, and she used my office on a couple of lunchbreaks to write emails and make some phone calls.'

'She didn't start chaining herself to excavators or railings?' asked Joyce.

'She had it in her, but no, it hadn't reached that point. No work has started because a sale hasn't gone through yet.'

'Maybe we should take a look?'

Ginger liked Joyce's suggestion. It was still a nice enough day to spend a couple more hours outside, and a visit to a historical building sounded a lot calmer than this morning's escapade.

Morton Hall was their second construction site of the day. At least, it looked like a construction site, but nothing was actually happening. A high chain-link fence circled the edge of the plot of land the building occupied between a large patch of tarmac that was being used as a carpark and a row of Georgian houses.

A black BMW was pulling out of the carpark and Ginger recognised John Bradbury behind the wheel. She grabbed Joyce and pointed in his direction. They watched him drive off down the road before venturing closer to the hall.

A couple of windows were boarded up and it looked as though it had been deserted for a long time. Ginger walked along the outside of the fence until she found a gap and squeezed through.

'Hey there, you can't come in here.' A slim man in an ill-fitting grey suit, hi-vis vest and hard hat was striding towards them. 'You need permission.'

'Can't you give us permission?' asked Ginger.

'Are you interested in buying the property?'

'I might be. Maybe you could show us around and we'll let you know if we want to buy it.'

He seemed to be considering the idea for a moment.

'No, sorry, you'd need to talk to the office and arrange a time through them. I can only take in the people whose names are on this list.'

'And John Bradbury's name is on the list? Oh, come on, we saw him drive off, we're not daft.'

'He has just been, yes.'

'He wants to buy it?'

'I can't tell you that.'

Ginger looked over at the house. 'You must have a lot of interest, it's beautiful.'

'It is. Some people think it should have listed status.'

'And others just want to turn it into a block of flats?'

'Something like that.' He smiled. 'Things have got a bit heated.'

'That must make things quite difficult for you.' Ginger shook her head as she spoke. If she could get him onside...

'It's certainly making things more challenging; it's all taking much longer than we expected and it's my first time working with a site like this.'

'I bet you'll be relieved when it's finally sold, even if it's to John Bradbury and he wants to knock it down and build a block of flats on the land.'

'Oh, he doesn't want to knock it down, but he does... No, I shouldn't be saying anything. I'm sorry, ladies, but I am going to have to ask you to leave now. You really shouldn't be in here.'

Ginger and Joyce smiled at him and did as he said. They had what they'd come for.

39

'Pass me the cream.'

Ginger reached out to the table on her side where the can of squirty cream sat and passed it to Joyce, who added another layer to her hot chocolate. She'd already eaten all her marshmallows. They were both in Ginger's bed, surrounded by the room's calming colours of deep burgundy red and cream. The king-size bed gave them both ample room to get comfortable with a mountain of cushions as they watched a film.

After a room-service dinner of cheeseburgers and chips followed by ice cream, which they'd eaten in the sitting room, they'd ordered hot chocolate with extra marshmallows. Both had then enjoyed a long, hot soak in their respective bathtubs before donning their pyjamas for the rest of the evening. A 'rom com' was in order and the best place to watch was from the comfort of the bed.

Joyce had relished sliding into her bubblegum-pink silk pyjamas with ivory piping and her initials monogrammed on a pocket. They had laughed when Ginger had come out of her room in ivory silk pyjamas of almost the exact same style. Hers had bubblegum-pink piping, but no monogram.

'Yin to my yang,' Joyce had declared. She'd fully expected to be greeted by enormously oversized fleece pyjamas covered in pictures of cats, and fluffy slippers that looked as if Ginger had stuck her feet up the bum of a pair of bright-pink hedgehogs. But no, Ginger was as elegant as she; in the sleepwear department, at least.

Joyce took a moment to wonder when she had last done something like this, a real 'girls' night'. It took a while, but she remembered it was with her sister, Bunny, even when they were well into their forties. Takeout dinner, probably fish and chips, a large bottle of Lambrusco, a family-sized box of Thornton's chocolates, and a film on the TV. Those were the days of the mad dash to the loo during the adverts with the other one shouting 'It's starting, it's starting!' if you weren't quick enough.

Joyce smiled to herself. Happy memories, but she missed her sister. Bunny had died of cancer far too young. The loss of a sibling was something she and Ginger had in common; Ginger's brother had also died before his time, killed in an arson attack.

Joyce shook herself out of what was turning into a melancholic train of thought and turned her attention back to the film. Feeling like a beached whale, she had nonetheless topped up the cream on her hot chocolate throughout the first half hour of *When Harry Met Sally*. When the chocolate was drained from the mug, she opted for more cream, using a teaspoon to consume it like a second dessert. She was not ashamed of her sweet tooth, especially not in front of Ginger. If they'd reached the point where they could have a pyjama party and share a bed to watch a movie, then unhealthy amounts of cream were perfectly acceptable.

'Any of that cream left?' Ginger asked as the credits rolled. 'If I ain't getting any *you know what,* then I'm going to make up for it with desserts and alcohol.' She emptied the remainder of the can into her mug and stole Joyce's teaspoon.

'Oh, come on, your time will come, just when you least expect it.' Joyce paused for a moment with an expression of befuddlement. 'This is a conversation I'd expect to be having with a teenager who's just been dumped, not a sixty-something, but if the platitudes fit.'

'Give over. You might still be on your search for Prince Charming, but I gave up on all that a long time ago. One broken heart is one too many in my book.'

'You give up too easily. That or they were pretty special.'

Ginger went quiet and Joyce knew it wasn't the time to try to get more information on why her friend was resolutely single. She took the canister of cream off her, gave it a hard shake and managed to get another couple of bursts out of it and into Ginger's mug. She was rewarded with a grateful smile.

'I've been thinking,' Ginger said as she wiped whipped cream off the end of her nose. 'Caroline seems like she was quite the determined woman. If she was prepared to take on a property developer like John Bradbury in order to prevent him getting his hands on a very valuable building, then not only does he remain a suspect, but there may well be other people that Caroline annoyed. I wonder if she's been involved in any other campaigns over the years.'

'We could talk to some other people fighting the developers. They might know if she's been involved in anything else, but don't forget, it's only the last two years. She was in London until then.'

'That's not a lot of time for her to make enemies. Especially if she was working hard and studying, added to which a lot of time would have been spent sorting out her mother's affairs when she first returned.' Ginger pulled a face.

'What was that for?' Joyce asked.

'I think the next course is a handful of indigestion tablets.'

'You're such an old woman. Stay there.' Joyce got up and went through to her room.

'You're older than I am,' Ginger called after her.

'I don't believe it, and anyway, you have no idea when I was born,' Joyce called back.

'Yes, I do. Two bottles of Moët and you were drunk enough to take out your passport, which was still in your handbag after you returned from your little sojourn to Majorca just after Christmas, so you could show off all your stamps.'

Joyce made a noise that could only be described as *harrumph* as she returned to the bedroom and passed Ginger a pack of Rennies.

'That was my fake passport in case I'm mugged and want to elicit sympathy from my mugger.'

Ginger muttered something very rude as she chewed on a tablet.

'How old were you when you retired?' Joyce asked her, thinking about age.

'I haven't, not really. I'm still taking in the occasional job, like Caroline's costume and the work I did for Dennis.'

'Okay then, when do you plan to retire?'

'My retirement plan is called death. Does that answer your question? Why? Having passed up the opportunity first time round, are you finally thinking about it? I was under the impression that they'd have to carry you out of Charleton House.'

'That's what I thought, too, but Dennis's comment about spending our retirement being mystery visitors to hotels – only the finest hotels, of course – got me thinking.'

'Well it would certainly save you a fortune in hotel bills. Are you really thinking about it?'

'No, not really.' Joyce lay back against the pillows and stared at the ceiling, wondering what it would be like to be a lady of leisure and away from spreadsheets, stocktakes, and staff members falling out and expecting her to play mother: a role she was not suited for. On the other hand, she had friends at Charleton House, and she enjoyed liaising with the Duchess and discussing new stock ideas. She felt honoured to work in such a beautiful, important building. A decision to leave was going to be a long, hard one that she wasn't ready to make yet.

'You know, we might be looking in the wrong place entirely,' Ginger said, chewing on a second indigestion tablet. 'The person with the opportunity for a more murky history here in Buxton was not Caroline, but her mother. She was the one who lived here until her death a couple of years ago, while Caroline had been away from home for a long time. Perhaps her mother did something or angered someone, and they decided to get revenge by killing Caroline as her mother was no longer an option.'

Joyce continued staring at the ceiling as she replied. 'There's something a bit "gangland" about a revenge killing. But it's not impossible. Dennis said Caroline's mother was a teacher, so it would be easy enough to find out where she worked and go and talk to someone who remembers her. So that's our plan for tomorrow, then?'

The response was a snore that could rattle windows. Joyce laughed to herself and got up, turned all the lights off and quietly pulled the door to.

40

'Good morning, ladieeees,' Dennis sang as they approached reception. 'How are you both on this beautiful Wednesday morning?'

Ginger looked down the corridor and out through the glass doors. It did indeed look rather bright and inviting. She assumed it was still cold, though, based on the scarves and gloves that people hurrying by outside were wearing.

'Starving, and in need of coffee,' she replied, staring at him with wide open eyes and an expression that she hoped said *don't get between me and my caffeine.*

'Good morning, Joyce, Ginger.' DS Harnby appeared behind Dennis from his office and stood in the doorway. 'Enjoying your stay?'

'Very much so,' Joyce answered. 'Very relaxing. Spas, fine wine.'

'No crosswords, jigsaws, or other forms of puzzles?' Harnby was looking at them intently, her head cocked to one side and a questing expression on her face.

'Oh no, that would be too much like hard work. Wouldn't it, Ginger?'

'Everything is hard work before coffee.' Just being polite was proving challenging to Ginger, even to a police officer.

'Now that's a nice colour.' Joyce was staring at Harnby's hands. Her fingernails were a vibrant crimson. Harnby glanced down.

'Bloody hell, I forgot all about that.'

'A pleasant night out, Detective Sergeant?' asked Dennis, unable to hide the amusement in his voice. Harnby sighed.

'I don't have the time to go home and remove it.'

'Why on earth would you want to remove it? It's a glorious colour.' Joyce sounded genuinely confused.

'Many reasons, one being a meeting with the Chief Inspector in an hour.'

'Stay right here,' Joyce ordered before striding off down the corridor at an impressive pace. Ginger's brain still wasn't awake so she didn't attempt small talk, and anyway, it was only a matter of minutes before Joyce reappeared and handed a bottle to Harnby.

'Nail polish remover, and here are some cotton wool pads. A shame to have to remove it, but if the occasion demands it, make sure you do it properly.'

'Well I never. Harnby has a saucy, fiery red-nail-polish-wearing alter ego.' Joyce looked rather smug. 'I need to remember that the next time she comes in dressed like an undertaker.'

Ginger's brain cells were being spurred into action by some very strong coffee. She was now awake enough to quiz Dennis about Harnby's visit.

'She asked me what I knew about Caroline's life down in London. It appears the police are starting to take some interest in that area of her life.'

'Interesting, that's something we can't look into. It's not like we can call up Scotland Yard and ask them to dig around,' Ginger commented. 'But it's good news if that means they are onto something.' Ginger was actually hoping that she and Joyce could find the killer before the police. There was no particular reason, just a sense of satisfaction in working it out faster than the professionals.

'Could you tell her much?'

'Hardly anything. The only London-related information I really know is that she got talking to Tim at an art gallery in Shoreditch. He had some work on display as part of a competition and Caroline was there to support one of the other artists. She recognised Buxton in one of Tim's paintings and told him she was about to move back up here. They talked, she mentioned she would be looking for work, wasn't fussy about what, and he told her about The Lodge, said to drop by in case I had anything available. The rest, as they say, is history. She had references from her previous work as a part-time librarian and history tutor, which were all excellent, so I gave her the job.'

Ginger nodded. 'We should give that more thought, but I'm too hungry to think. I need food.'

'I certainly don't want to get between you and your breakfast. I learnt a very long time ago that can only result in you taking a chunk out of my arm, or whatever fleshy limb is closest. I'm sure I have a few teeth marks from when you've been desperate. Please leave a little for the other guests.'

As Joyce tucked in to poached eggs on avocado toast, Ginger devoured her full English. She was surprised at just how hungry she was, despite the double cheeseburger and mountain of thick-cut chips she had enjoyed last night. Her mother had often joked that she had worms and was forever grateful that rationing had ended four years before Ginger was born.

'Ginger,' Joyce interrupted her thoughts, 'over at the bar.' Graham Bennett had walked in and was talking to Dennis. A large crease was carved across his forehead as he scribbled notes. Eventually, Dennis left him to it.

'Grab another seat,' Joyce instructed Ginger before getting up and making her way over to Graham. After a brief conversation, he followed her back. 'I thought Graham might like a cup of coffee before he starts work,' Joyce said casually.

'Good morning, Graham, you must be almost finished now.' Ginger reached for a spare cup and saucer off a nearby table.

'I am. Just a few little things here and there. A couple of small repair jobs where things got knocked as furniture was returned to the rooms.'

'What next?' Joyce asked as she poured him a cup of coffee. 'You're clearly in demand, you must be fighting people off.'

He smiled awkwardly. 'You could say that. But I don't want to overwork the team. What are your plans for today? Some shopping? A visit to the museum?' He seemed keen to change the subject, but Ginger wasn't having any of it.

'So, what do you have lined up next? If you're doing more and more work of a historic nature, you must have some very interesting jobs coming up.'

Graham took his time adding sugar to his coffee and taking his first drink.

'Well, there's another hotel towards Macclesfield that will keep me busy, a few private houses, then I'm lined up to do some work at Charleton House.'

Ginger watched Joyce try to hide a look of surprise.

'Charleton House? Well, that *is* something to be proud of. What will you be doing there?'

'It's not a big job, I've been asked to work on… well… repair some… there are some banisters that need some rather delicate repair work.' Ginger glanced across at Joyce, who gave her a look of confusion.

He can't know that Joyce works there, Ginger thought.

'Who are you going to be working with?' Joyce asked, before quickly adding, 'I know a few people who work there.'

Graham paused.

'I forget the name. Older man, erm...'

'Peter?' suggested Joyce.

'That's it, Peter. Well, ladies, thank you for the coffee, but I really ought to crack on. Only got a couple of days to get this place finished, and the manager is a real slave driver.' He laughed nervously and left the room.

'Peter?' asked Ginger.

'Made him up.' Joyce picked up her phone and found the name she was looking for in her contacts.

'Robert, darling, how are you on this fine day?... Glad to hear it. Now, I have a question for you. You deal with contractors for the maintenance team, don't you?' She nodded as she listened. 'Marvellous. Now, have you any work lined up with a Graham Bennett, a carpenter?' She sipped at her coffee as she listened, Ginger watching her expression change so often, she had no idea what Joyce was being told. 'Thank you, Robert, that's very useful. Now, before I go, can I check your lads have my counter top in the courtyard shop near the very top of their to-do list, if not at the actual top? I'll be back on Monday at the latest and... My dear Robert, I could kiss you.'

Joyce roared with laughter and hung up. 'Well, old girl,' she said between guffaws, 'the mystery continues. Robert knows Graham, but hasn't offered him any work and can't see why he would need to for the foreseeable future.'

'So why would he lie to us? Dennis has said that he's very popular and he has a team of men working with him.'

'Where are they? They're certainly not here.' Joyce looked around the room in a mock search.

'On another job? If Graham only has the loose ends to sort out, then he would surely send his team off to get started on the next job. That's assuming that his other jobs are all real. Or even if they're a figment of his imagination. Mind you, he didn't look happy when we saw him with John Bradbury. Maybe that job has fallen through, if it ever existed. I could talk to Dennis about it all. He might have an idea what's going on. Good morning, Mrs Dalrymple.'

Ginger's greeting to the elderly woman as she walked past was returned with a broad smile.

'Well, hello there. I must say, you always look so cheerful in the morning. And your blouse…' She was looking at Joyce. 'It doesn't matter what the weather is outside, I feel like you've brought summer with you.'

She patted Joyce's arm as she returned to her husband at the table behind them. The round splotches of colour on Joyce's blouse looked to Ginger as though Kandinsky had practised on her before having his morning coffee.

'Personally, I thought a unicorn had vomited on you.'

The smile on Joyce's face was replaced swiftly with a scowl.

41

With breakfast finished and the first barbed comment of the day delivered by Ginger, the two women returned to reception where Dennis was saying goodbye to a guest who had just checked out.

'I hope you ladies are both satiated. Joyce, is that a Kandinsky or a Paul Klee?' Dennis looked at Joyce's top, although she couldn't tell if he was admiring it or if she should expect a unicorn-vomit-related follow-up.

'We have a question for you...'

'I need to speak to a manager,' asked an unfamiliar voice from beside them.

'That's me, madam. How can I help?'

'My phone has been stolen. I had it with me at breakfast, but it's gone. Everything is on there, I can't lose it. I just can't.'

As Joyce and Ginger stepped back, remaining within earshot, Joyce spotted a familiar figure walk past the door to the hotel. Telling Ginger to hang on in case she heard anything useful, she stepped outside. Joyce didn't have a coat on, but it wasn't actually that cold. Even so, she didn't want to stay outside any longer than was necessary.

'Lydia, have you got a minute?' Clearly on her way to the spa, her white uniform visible, hanging below her short bomber jacket, Lydia smiled.

'Of course. Joyce, right?'

'You remembered.'

'You're not easy to forget.' Joyce laughed; she took any comment along those lines as a compliment. 'How can I help?'

'I have a question.'

'Oh yes?'

'How much do you know about John's attempt to buy Morton Hall on the Manchester Road?'

'I know some, it's a project close to his heart.'

'Do you know about Caroline fighting for its preservation?'

'Of course. John's project has a lot of critics, it's been in the local press. Not just him, there's a bigger company that wants to buy the hall, too, and a plot of land behind it. They've been getting even more criticism. I know Caroline was at those meetings, she appeared in a couple of photos when the papers covered them.'

'So, John knew all about her role?'

'Well, he knew she was interested, but so were a lot of people. He probably saw her at the meetings.'

'I get the feeling she was taking a *lot* of interest. She'd been asking questions of people involved.' Joyce wasn't going to tell Lydia about Caroline's notes.

'I didn't realise that, I think I viewed her as a bit of a passionate academic type. I didn't think of her as someone who would get her hands dirty. That would really upset John.'

Joyce was starting to feel the cold. 'Okay, thanks.'

'Has something happened?' Lydia looked a little concerned.

'No, no. I should get back in.'

'Do, you look frozen. If you have any time later, I have a couple of slots free, you should come in for a massage. I'll get you a discount.'

Lydia smiled sweetly and carried on down the street. Joyce dashed for the hotel door.

Ginger was still at the reception desk when Joyce returned. The woman whose phone had been stolen had gone.

'Everything alright?' asked Joyce as she tried to tuck herself around the corner of the desk, close to a radiator. 'Has the phone been found?'

Dennis shook his head. 'I've asked her to double-check her room and retrace her steps this morning, but she's convinced she had it with her at breakfast. I don't understand how it could have been stolen from under her nose, though.'

'She'll probably find she left it in the bathroom,' Ginger agreed. 'It seems to me that these days, most people can't even go for a pee without taking their phone with them, and I bet half of them are forever leaving it in there. So unhygienic.'

'Did you ask him more about Caroline's mother?' Joyce asked Ginger. She had now taken to perching on the radiator.

'You'll get piles, and no, I haven't had a chance.'

'Her mother?' asked Dennis. 'What do you want to know?'

'Well, for a start, her name would be useful,' said Joyce. 'We can't spend our time asking about someone known only to us as *Caroline's mother*.'

'Well, yes to that,' agreed Ginger, 'but do you know where she taught? We think it's time we found out more about her.'

'Okay, well, Dorothy Clatworthy was the head teacher at a school here in Buxton: St John's Secondary School. Started as a history teacher and worked her way up. Caroline once told me that it was hell being the head teacher's daughter; she was bullied quite a lot for it, although she was able to laugh about it later.'

'Did she talk about her mother much?'

'Not really, but that's not unusual. I don't, unless she's done something to irritate me.'

'Are you talking about Caroline's mum?' Barbara Dwyer, the receptionist, had arrived. 'My sister's a dinner lady at St John's, has been for forty years. She could tell you a tale or two, and some of them about Dorothy.'

'Anything you can tell us?'

'She was strict, that I do know; nothing got past her and she was forever doling out detentions. She was very tall and had jet black hair. Even as she got older, there wasn't a spot of grey, but no one thought she dyed it. Which is ridiculous, but I think some of them thought she was some kind of witch. Most of the kids were scared of her, but everyone I know who was taught by her would look back and say she was brilliant at her job. Guess you just needed an adult perspective on it all. Gillian, my sister, said that Mrs Clatworthy loved the kids, despite the gruff exterior, and she'd fight for them if she thought they were in trouble. She was someone you wanted on your side.'

Joyce thought there was something familiar about the description.

'I remember it all kicked off when a whole family was put into care. Four kids and the mum was looking after them on her own, only she couldn't cope. When the school called social services and they were fostered, there was a bit of a mixed response. Some said it was the right thing to do, some said they should never 'ave been separated. I don't know all the ins and outs so I can't say for sure, but I do know Mrs Clatworthy got blamed by those who felt it was wrong, even though she was just doing her job. Gillian said it showed how much she cared; she knew something had to be done, even if it was a difficult decision.'

'What happened to the children, do you know?' Ginger asked.

'No idea, it was years ago. I could always ask Gillian, she might have more information.'

'Thank you, but we'll be able to find out more.' Joyce stood up, convinced she could smell burning coming from around her legs. 'Ginger, fancy a drive down memory lane? The smell of boiled cabbage and sweaty gym kit, and the swirl of chalk dust in the air?'

'I think you'll find it's all electronic gadgetry now. Shame really, I always liked being given the job of cleaning off the blackboard at the end of the day.'

'Is that a yes or a no?'

'Yes, Miss, absolutely, of course. Please don't put me in detention, Miss.'

Joyce gave her a gentle shove down the corridor.

'Come on then, Salt, get your coat. And don't dawdle.'

42

'What is it about schools that always sends a shiver down my spine?' Joyce was giving St John's a once-over while Ginger found somewhere to park.

'I find it hard to picture you at school. The closest I can get is you at your current age, wearing some sort of schoolgirl's uniform with a short skirt, using the tie as a belt, and a shirt that is criminally tight.' Ginger was only half joking. The idea of Joyce in a school uniform took her mind to places she didn't want to go, but she really did find it a challenge to think of Joyce as a *youth*.

'You'd be hard pressed to find a teacher who remembers me. Let's just say I didn't have the most impressive of attendance records.'

'You were always up to no good with Derbyshire's answer to Danny Zuko?'

'You're showing your age if a young John Travolta in *Grease* is the best you can come up with!' snorted Joyce. 'Anyway, I never had the chance. Bunny and I were in so many schools, I hardly had the time to learn the name of the local heartthrob. Mum did her best and we went to school as much as possible, but she was on the road most of the time. And we were fine, the three of us. We got on with things and we both turned out perfectly alright. More than alright, in fact, as I'm sure you'll agree.'

Ginger did, honestly. Joyce's mum, a Tiller girl who toured the country with her dance troupe, had done a fantastic job.

'Right, let's see what sort of harridan runs the school office. This place is rather gloomy.'

The long two-storeyed Victorian building was made of stone so dark, it was almost black. To one side, a row of Portakabins stood in a line. School grounds always seemed eerie when there wasn't a child to be seen. Ginger knew they'd all be in class, but not a single one was dashing to their next lesson, or running an errand. If the head teacher was continuing in the vein of Dorothy Clatworthy, then there probably wasn't a lot of lateness.

A small wooden sign painted burgundy red with gold lettering pointed the way to the office through a small archway. Inside, the main school building was as sombre as Ginger had pictured with dark wood walls and ceiling. Through another set of doors was a lobby with a glass window to their right. Ginger rang a bell next to the window and a woman appeared as if she had spent the morning waiting expressly for this moment.

'Can I help?'

'Oh, er, yes.' Ginger had to gather her thoughts after the surprise of the jack-in-the-box receptionist. 'We'd like to talk to someone who remembers Dorothy Clatworthy, the old head teacher.'

'Can I ask why?'

'It's a personal matter.'

'I'll have to see if there is...'

'Faye, can I help?' A tall man in a navy-blue V-neck sweater appeared in the window. 'I'm Dominic Cross, history teacher. I was here for Dorothy's final couple of years in post, so I might be able to assist. Head through those doors, turn right and I'll meet you in the corridor.'

Following the man's directions, they were greeted by a warm smile and firm handshake before Dominic Cross walked them further down the corridor to his classroom. Two walls were covered in world maps: political, economic and the routes of famous explorers. Another wall had the headline 'Medieval and Renaissance Medicine' and a variety of information sheets pinned underneath it. Lord Kitchener stared at them from the fourth wall and made it very clear just how much he wanted them. Next to him, Rosie the Riveter reminded them they could do it.

'I'm not teaching this period so we won't be disturbed. Now, what do you need to know about Dorothy, and does this by any chance have something to do with the death of her daughter?' He had offered them chairs, but they opted to sit on the desks at the front of the room, as he had sat on the front of his own desk. Ginger spotted a cycling helmet sitting on a bag in the corner; he clearly kept himself fit. There was no malice in his expression, just genuine curiosity.

'It is. We've been trying to find out about her, but we realised that it might be important to know more about her mother too.'

'And why might you be keen to know more?'

Ginger looked quickly across at Joyce, but saw no signs of concern.

'She worked, and died, at my friend's hotel. The staff are like family there, and he wants to know what happened as soon as possible. People have a tendency to open up to a pair of harmless old women.'

Dominic smiled. 'I doubt that either of you is entirely harmless, and we're probably not that dissimilar in age, so I wouldn't say old either. But I can't see why talking to you would do any harm. So, what exactly do you want to know about Dorothy?'

'We were wondering if she might have left behind some enemies. We heard about a case of a family being put into care, which I can imagine upset a few people. Was that a one-off or did she get involved in a lot of contentious events?'

'The thing you need to understand about Dorothy is she would have done anything for the children at the school, even if that meant making some very, *very* tough decisions. But she would have been the wrong person for the job if she hadn't. The case you mentioned is a particularly severe one; it happened in my first year here, so I saw first-hand how difficult things were.

'There were four children living with their mother. The father was in and out of prison, and when he was around, he was no good. I'm pretty sure the children felt the sharp end of his temper more than once. The mother couldn't cope and they lived in a dreadful place, the children often came to school hungry, their clothes unwashed. Mrs Jenks, the maths teacher, used to take their clothes home to wash for them, sending them home in clean things from the lost-property box. We made sure they were fed during the day, but they didn't always turn up.'

'Were the children separated?'

'Yes, sort of. They were split into pairs and fostered that way, so they still had one of their siblings with them.'

'What happened to them in the end?' Joyce asked softly.

'Not sure. Two of them moved schools to somewhere closer to the family they were placed with. The ones that remained here, I really don't know, other than they left school when they reached sixteen. I didn't teach them, but they were certainly around for a while. I guess that over time, they just became part of the general melee and didn't stand out. I would imagine that attendance remained an issue.'

'Was there anything else that Dorothy was involved with?'

'No, nothing that would stand out as different to the usual issues a head teacher has to deal with, many of them challenging and sometimes heartbreaking. But that is the most memorable one. There is a retired teacher who might know what happened to the children. Frank Flagg – he's in a home now, getting on a bit, but still got all his marbles. If there's anyone who'll remember, it's him.'

Dominic made a note on a piece of paper and handed it over. 'Tell him I sent you and that I'll be over next week. He likes craft beer and I make a monthly visit with some new ones I've found.' He stood. 'Is there anything else I can help you with? A quick overview of 1066? The Battle of Fulford, perhaps, or Stamford Bridge? No? Good, not my favourites. Give my best to Frank, and I hope you find what it is you need.'

43

*J*oyce offered to visit Frank by herself; it didn't need two of them and she thought that Ginger might appreciate some time with Dennis. After giving the inside of Ginger's car a good wipe down, she took a fifteen-minute drive out to The Cedars, a residential home for the elderly. It was a large, imposing building tucked away behind some trees and set in its own grounds, but was less austere looking than the school they had just been to. All the same, it wouldn't have surprised her to discover it had been a school back in the day.

An elderly chap in the big bay window gave her a wave. It turned out he was Frank.

'I thought things had perked up around here when I saw you walk up the path, but I didn't think you'd want to see me. What have I done to deserve this? Is it my birthday?' He gave Joyce a very obvious once-over. She was waiting with an impatient look on her face when his eyes met hers.

'Hey, what do you expect? It's not like we have someone like you here every day. The staff here are all very nice, but it's good to have a bit of variety.'

She laughed, appreciating his honesty. 'Well, let's hope your memory is as good as your eyesight. Dominic Cross said you might be able to help.'

'When's he coming round? He owes me a beer.'

'Next week, said something about some craft beer.'

'Good lad. You know, I don't envy him. Teaching is all paperwork and testing nowadays. I was lucky and retired before all that turned teachers from educators into paper-pushing bureaucrats. It's not their fault, and many still do a great job, but it's not what it was. But you ain't here so I can drone on about all that. What do you need my memory for?' He settled back in his chair, his hands on his lap.

'Dorothy Clatworthy. What do you remember about a family of four children who went into care?'

His face softened. 'Oh my, that is a while back. Very sad, it was. She faced a lot of criticism for all that, but it was absolutely the right thing to do. I have no doubt about that.'

'Do you know what happened to the children? Did they stay in the area?'

'I couldn't tell you, love. Two left the school not long after and the other two left as soon as they could a couple of years later. I spent quite a lot of time with one of the boys, Thomas. It was anybody's guess whether he'd actually bother to come in or not, but he was almost always there for my classes. Good thing, too; he had talent.'

'What did you teach?'

'Art.'

'What did you say his name was?'

'Thomas. Thomas Stafford. I might even have some of his work; I have a chest full of students' art at my son's house. I kept the best of the work that students didn't collect at the end of the year, just in case they changed their mind, and because I was proud of them. Sentimental old fool. I can ask him to have a look, if you'd like? He's visiting this evening.'

Joyce wasn't sure what good it would do, but said yes and gave Frank her phone number.

'Thank you, Frank.'

'You're not going, are you? Come on, have a cup of tea with me. Game of cards? If for no other reason than to make all the other chaps jealous. We'll take a photograph and I can tell our Jim that he's getting a new stepmother.'

That made Joyce laugh out loud and accept his offer. 'I'm not much of a card player.'

'Scrabble, then, and I won't be gentle with you.'

'Do I look like someone who has to be allowed to win?'

He gave her another once-over. 'You look like someone who's going to wipe the floor with me. How about you go easy on me?'

'Not a chance.' Joyce was not a woman who liked to be beaten. Not even by an OAP in a care home. The gloves were off.

44

'*D*id you win?' Ginger asked as they walked down the corridor towards their suite.

'No. We played best out of three and the old sod won. I tell you, he went for the jugular with WHEEZILY, which I suggested came to mind because it's how he climbs the stairs these days.'

'Ouch, how did he take that?'

'Not well. It wasn't long before he got JEZEBEL and took a great deal of pleasure asking me if I had any observations to make about *that* word.'

'Sounds like you met your match.'

'Not quite so fast, I'm going again next week to see if I can even things up.'

Ginger hadn't thought of Joyce as the kind of woman who would make visits to people she barely knew in old folks' homes, unless they were likely to be stinking rich with no heirs.

'Do you think that this Thomas Stafford is someone worth chasing up?' Joyce asked.

'Definitely, we should have another look at Caroline's notes and see if we've missed a reference in there. We could ask

Madeleine if Caroline mentioned the name, and I'll check with Dennis. But it's so long ago, I'm not sure how far we'll get. Not only was Dorothy retired, but she's dead.'

'You know, I was thinking.' Joyce looked a little unsure about whatever it was she was going to say next. 'Thomas was meant to be an exceptional art student. Frank was telling me that he'd gone as far as gathering application forms for a number of art colleges in the hope that Thomas would apply. Anyway, art. It's not easy to think about, but what if...'

A door flew open and almost hit Ginger in the face.

'What the...?' She staggered back and Joyce grabbed her, keeping her upright. Marjorie Dalrymple appeared from behind the door and smiled when she saw the two women.

'Oh, I am sorry, are you alright? I just needed some clean towels.'

She walked off down the corridor, humming to herself. Joyce and Ginger stuck their heads around the door. Shelves were filled floor to ceiling with towels and bed linen.

'Can I get you ladies anything?' Helen had appeared behind them; she sounded a little concerned.

'No, thank you,' replied Joyce. 'Although it seems you aren't providing Mrs Dalrymple with enough towels.'

Helen laughed. 'I'm used to that. She comes and helps herself from time to time. Just one of the quirks we've got used to over the months. We view her a bit like an extension of the team; we've found her in the kitchen boiling herself some eggs and behind the bar when she has the urge for an afternoon sherry and the bar staff have stepped away for a moment. Are you sure I can't get you anything?'

Both women replied no and continued on their way, Ginger hoping that she had as much character when she was Mrs Dalrymple's age. She liked to picture herself behind a bar, helping herself and using her advancing years as a get out of jail free card.

· · ·

Following an afternoon that found Ginger taking a nap and Joyce enjoying a long soak in the bath, they decided it was time to venture out again and opted for a pub on the far side of Buxton that had a reputation for excellent curries. They were starting to feel as if they were taking advantage of Dennis's generosity, and curry was something that Dennis admitted his chefs never put on their menu.

They settled themselves in a corner of the pub, partially hidden behind a traditional glass and wood partition, but still with a good view of the bar, and chose korma, madras, saag paneer, a couple of naan breads and a portion of rice to share. While they waited, they both ordered gin and tonics.

'I miss these places,' Ginger said. 'There were trendy wine bars in the 80s, and now it's all craft beers and young men with beards that need a good trim. I like an old-fashioned pub where you can get a pint of bitter and a packet of pork scratchings.'

'And you stick to the floor and can smell the men's urinals at fifty yards. Oh yes, those were the days.'

'Don't be such a misery, these are the places of our misspent youth. I remember my old pa used to head down the pub every Friday night to meet the lads. He wasn't one of those men who disappeared *every* night, but Friday nights were his. Saturday night was always reserved for the family. Your father must have been the same; they would have been similar ages and from the same area.'

'No idea. Only met him a handful of times. My maternal grandfather could always be found in the pub, though, propping the bar up with a pint in his hand. A man of few words, as I remember.'

The food arrived, the plates and bowls filling the small table. Ginger inhaled deeply.

'It's been far too long since I had a good curry.'

It tasted as good as it smelt.

'I'm not sure we're getting anywhere,' Ginger said as she

chewed on a piece of naan, the warm bread dipped in the korma sauce. 'John is pretty suspect, he has a number of motives. I'm beginning to wonder if there is a link with Dorothy and the school, we've got the thefts, but nothing is really standing out. Maybe that "aha" moment is really a myth. It's not going to suddenly hit us and we'll end up in a car chase through the hills of the Peak District, or one of us will get held hostage and the other will have to rescue them using a headscarf and a bag of mints. We're more likely to end up under arrest for getting in DS Harnby's way.'

'Oh, ye of little faith. I agree, the school is worth pursuing and I'm convinced there is something about those thefts at The Lodge that is particularly fishy. It may well be fishy enough for Caroline to be murdered over.'

'Do you think it's Helen or Ed?' Ginger asked.

'Not Ed, no. He knows something; he's worried, afraid even, but he's not the killer. Helen, on the other hand... I don't think she's afraid of getting her hands dirty, literally or metaphorically. She's got the look of a crazed lioness.'

Ginger nodded. 'She's always been very nice, but every time I've met her, I've felt like I wouldn't want to cross her. There's a look in her eyes – I don't know how to describe it, but there's a hardness there.'

'Hang on, speak of the devil. Or the devil's offspring.' Joyce was looking over at the bar where Ed had just been handed a pint of amber liquid. He took a drink, and then acknowledged a lad of a similar age who stood next to him. After a brief chat Ed handed him something, but the row of tap handles hid what it was.

Joyce and Ginger ate in silence for a little while, only paying attention to the world around them when the young man Ed had spoken to at the bar walked past their table and joined a group of friends. They were close enough to hear his comment as he sat down.

'Barely used, but he's asking too much. It's the same model as mine; I want something newer.' He looked at his mobile phone. 'I'm not going to bother.'

Joyce and Ginger looked at one another. Joyce was the first to speak.

'He might not be a killer, but he's handling stolen goods. What next?'

'We finish this curry. After that, we need to talk to Dennis. I have a good idea what's going on.' Ginger fished a chunk of paneer out of the saag before looking back at Joyce. 'Now tell me if I'm crazy, but I reckon that...'

---

45

*J*oyce did think her friend was crazy, but that was a general state of affairs and not dependent on Ginger's views on the thefts. She had initially thought that Ginger's explanation was leaning in the utterly insane direction, but it gradually reduced to bonkers, then not impossible. By the time Ginger had finished, Joyce was largely on board, although she was still hedging her bets just a little.

'I know you looked at who was working at the time of each theft, but did you check who was staying?'

Dennis had taken one end of the sofa in their suite, after finding the taxidermied squirrel in the cupboard and putting it back on the shelf.

'Do you mean guests? Briefly, but not in great detail. We have regulars, but the chances of them being here every time are slim. Besides which, the only people who have access to all the rooms are staff.'

'But are they?' asked Ginger in a heavy, mysterious tone that verged on the comic detective. If she had been wearing glasses, Ginger would now be peering over them to ask that everyone be gathered in the library. Not that The Lodge had one.

'My darling Ginger, I know when you're up to something; you start stringing me along with an inappropriate amount of pleasure. Any chance you could get to your no doubt earth-shattering point?'

Ginger briefly pouted like a small child. 'I think that it is indeed one of your guests. If there's a slight disparity between the dates they stayed and the number of thefts, it is probably because someone else – a staff member, perhaps – got it into their head that it was clearly easy to do and swiped a couple of things themselves. Maybe they then lost their nerve, or were amongst your temporary staff so weren't here for very long. Also, at least one of your staff *is* involved.'

'So was it staff or wasn't it? You're losing me.' Dennis looked at Joyce as if she might have the answers. She'd only partially understood Ginger's theory herself, so she wasn't going to take over.

'Your delightful, slightly confused, sweet old guest, Marjorie Dalrymple, is a little more switched on than you might think, and she's your crack thief. She wanders around without anyone paying much attention, *"accidentally"'* Ginger made air quotes with her fingers 'wandering into other people's rooms when the cleaner is working in the bathroom or otherwise distracted. She can bump into people, stop at their table and chat – which is probably what happened this morning, by the way. Mrs Dalrymple puts her morning paper over the phone, chats for a couple of minutes, then picks up the paper and the phone and toddles off on her way. A little while later, the owner of the phone realises it's missing, but has no idea how.

'Mrs Dalrymple passes the stolen item on to *Helen*, either when they just "happen"', more air quotes, 'to run into each other in the park', or when she leaves it in the linen closet. Helen then sells it. I imagine they're splitting the profits.'

Dennis sat back with such force and a great gasp of air, which sounded as if he'd been knocked backwards by a punch.

'Why would she do something like that? She's an old woman.'

'Old women can still be thieves. Maybe it's something she's always done. Maybe she's bored and wants a bit of excitement in her life. Maybe she has health problems which result in her doing extreme things. It could be all of the above.'

'And Helen? She's a hard worker.'

'It seems she works hard at a lot of things,' Joyce said. Dennis sat in silence for a couple of minutes.

'I have often thought that Mr Dalrymple seems overly watchful of his wife, like he's afraid she's going to do something. He's always wanting to know where she is and only leaves her on her own when she's napping…'

'Or he thinks she's napping.'

'Quite, Joyce. I wonder if he knows.'

'How are you going to find that out? You can hardly stride up to him in the bar, ask him if he's having a pleasant stay and say, "Oh, by the way, did you know your wife's a kleptomaniac?"'

'Well, I don't know what else I can do, Ginger. I don't just want to call the police without knowing more. I'll have to try and find a way of working out what he knows, see if he'll open up to me.'

'Good luck with that.' Joyce couldn't imagine a man less likely to reveal his inner concerns.

'You haven't told anyone else, have you?'

'No,' Ginger confirmed. 'And if you want, we can leave this with you now. I'll talk to the police or anyone else you want, but we won't do anything without your say-so. We still have to get to the bottom of Caroline's death.'

Dennis wasn't his usual cheerful self as he left the room. He looked as though he was still trying to put together all the jigsaw pieces that Ginger had laid before him and he couldn't quite comprehend the picture that was forming.

'Thanks,' he said just before he closed the door, 'I think.'

Joyce and Ginger had concluded that they hadn't had enough to drink at the pub, so Ginger raided the mini bar. Neither of them felt like going out to the hotel bar; they didn't want to run into Mr and Mrs Dalrymple, and they weren't sure what they'd say if they saw Helen.

'We must tell Dennis to talk to Ed as soon as possible,' Ginger blurted out. 'If he didn't manage to sell the phone in the pub, then he'll still have it and it can be reunited with its owner.'

'I guess there's a silver lining,' Joyce said. She had been wondering if she'd been entirely wrong about Ed and he was more involved than she had thought, but she always came to the same conclusion. 'I think we might have witnessed Ed's first attempt to sell stolen goods.'

'What makes you think that?' Ginger had started a game of patience on the coffee table.

'He always seems really worried, on edge. I suspect he's realised what his mother is doing and is very concerned. He doesn't want to call the police on his own mother, and now we've started asking questions, I think he tried to sell the phone tonight to get rid of it as soon as possible and remove any link to her. If he was more experienced, then he would have gone further afield, not to a pub fifteen minutes' walk away. I can't imagine that anyone with any sense would try to sell stolen goods while stood at the bar; it's not very discreet. The poor lad isn't thinking straight.'

'Hmmm.' Ginger moved more cards.

'You look like you're killing time.'

'I am.'

'Why, what are you waiting for? We could put on a film or read a book.'

'I've no idea. It's like we're about to find out something, or I'm waiting until tomorrow when we get back on the trail of Caroline's killer. I can't think about anything else.'

'I know what you mean. It has rather taken over.'

There was a gentle tap on the door. Joyce stood up and went over to open it, to Dennis and Mr Dalrymple.

46

*G*inger stood, and then indicated the sofa to the two men. 'Can I get you a drink?' she offered; the men declined. Mr Dalrymple seemed as upright and composed as always, but he looked pale. He sat squarely on the edge of the sofa, although Ginger doubted he really knew what relaxation was even at the best of times.

'After we spoke,' Dennis explained, 'I talked to Mr Dalrymple. I decided that honesty and openness were important as I have come to think of both him and his wife as part of The Lodge family. I thought you might like to know what Mr Dalrymple has to say, and he was keen to talk to you himself. Isn't that right?' He spoke the last sentence particularly softly.

'Indeed. I have always wondered when this day would come. You see, I did everything I could to stop it happening. I love my wife dearly and never wanted her to get into trouble. I have spoken to her a number of times, but she continues to persist in her... activities.'

As he paused, Joyce took the opportunity to speak to him.

'Are you sure we can't get you a drink?'

'Actually, a scotch would be rather pleasant.'

'Phone the bar, they know what Mr Dalrymple drinks. In fact, tell them to bring the bottle and four glasses.'

Joyce nodded her thanks at Dennis and made the call. When she returned to the group, she sat on the arm of the chair that Ginger had chosen. Mr Dalrymple continued.

'Many years into our marriage, I discovered that my wife had a criminal record. Nothing too serious. Youthful indiscretions. A few things stolen from shops as part of dares between friends, nothing more. I didn't give it a moment's thought until a couple of years ago.

'We had been staying in a hotel in Torquay and a few small items had gone missing. A couple of little ornaments, a letter opener. I thought nothing of it. Last year, Dennis, you started to experience a few things being taken from here. Again, I thought little of it. We'd been coming here for quite a long time at that point and there hadn't been a problem before, not that I was aware of. Then, when I was packing for us to return home after a visit, I found a mobile phone in a drawer. I don't know if you recall, Dennis, but I handed it in, thinking that a previous guest of that room had left it behind.

'The next visit, I found one of those electronic books. I left it where it was, asked Marjorie about it, and when I returned to retrieve it later, it had gone. Every time we stayed after that, another guest reported that something had gone missing, and eventually I put two and two together.'

A loud knock at the door disturbed his flow and Joyce went to collect the bottle of scotch, four glasses and a bucket of ice on a tray. She poured large servings and handed them around.

'I'm most grateful, thank you,' Mr Dalrymple said before taking a drink and continuing. 'Marjorie denied any involvement, but I just knew. I tried to ensure that I never left her side and for a while it stopped. But I couldn't be with her every moment; she's a grown woman and I am not her keeper. I thought about telling someone, but I couldn't bring myself to report her to the authorities. She has been a dedicated mother and wife, and now a wonderful grandmother.

'I realise I have not always been the easiest of husbands. For a very long time, my work had to come first and she was left raising the family. Not a very exciting life; it was what was expected, but I know she wanted more. I know that I can appear rather...' he paused and thought for a moment '...stiff, perhaps, a little detached, but I love my wife very much. She has remained loyal to me, and I to her.'

Ginger didn't want to interrupt. She understood how difficult this must be for him. She placed him in his eighties, so he wasn't from the generation of men to open up. It was doubtful he had male friends who he went to the pub with; he more likely met people to discuss politics or sat on committees for the local rotary club. He was probably tired and worried and simply trying to keep his wife safe. But, she did have a question which wasn't easy to ask.

'Mr Dalrymple, have you ever thought that this might be a sign of something else? That she might need some medical help?'

'I suspect you are referring to dementia. It has crossed my mind, but this isn't a pint of milk here or there that she forgot she had in her hand. However, it is perhaps time to seek help in case it is caused by something else.'

'What about Helen? You knew she was involved?'

He nodded at Ginger. 'I did. It was her suggestion; she had worked out that it was Marjorie and spoke to me about it. I was never sure whether she intended to tell you, Dennis, or the police, but it didn't feel like a threat when she proposed her suggestion, although I have no doubt that would have come next. Marjorie has never needed the money, so she would pass the items on to Helen who would dispose of them, keeping the money, although I know that Marjorie did ask that she spend it on her children's education. This approach satisfied everyone's needs.'

For a little while, there was nothing but the sound of ice cubes clinking in glasses. Ginger preferred bourbon to scotch, but scotch seemed somehow more appropriate for this moment. Helen's approach might have satisfied both her and Mrs Dalrymple's needs, but it was hardly fair on the people who'd lost items of value, nor on Dennis whose reputation could easily have suffered as a result. The upright gentleman before her had in effect condoned his wife's criminal tendencies. She and Joyce had solved the mystery of the thefts, but Ginger didn't feel an ounce of satisfaction. She wished now that she didn't know.

'What will you do?' Mr Dalrymple's voice was soft but steady as he directed his question at Dennis. To Ginger's ear, it sounded as though he simply wanted to know what would happen next in order to prepare for it. He didn't sound afraid of the answer; there was no pleading in his voice.

'I don't know, Mr Dalrymple. You're due to check out on Saturday morning, it's now Wednesday night. Let me think about the situation and I will tell you by Friday evening. But please, promise me that between now and then there will be no more thefts, or I will have to go straight to the police and tell them all we know.'

Mr Dalrymple placed his glass on the table and slowly stood.

'Thank you, to you all for your time. Dennis, thank you for being so understanding. I will ensure that Marjorie doesn't have the opportunity to do any further damage and I will await your decision. Goodnight, ladies.'

Following a rather formal bow, he left the room.

here was silence, until Ginger gave a great exhalation of air and reached for the bottle of scotch.

'Well, that was blooming awful. What do we do now?'

'I don't think there is anything else for you and me to do,' replied Joyce. 'Dennis, we have to leave this in your hands now. It's a very difficult situation, especially if it is something that Mrs Dalrymple isn't fully able to control, but if that is the case, then it is time she got help.'

Dennis rubbed his fingers across his eyes. 'If I tell the police, then I also need to tell them about Helen. She has worked for me for a very long time; she was one of the first people I recruited after becoming general manager. She's always been the hardest-working member of staff and supported me through every change, every challenge.'

'She's also been betraying your trust all this time.' Ginger said what, Joyce assumed, Dennis had been getting to in his own time.

'Yes.' He hadn't looked at either of them yet; he seemed to be staring right though the coffee table as though it simply wasn't there. 'I dread to think what this will do to the rest of the team. Everyone looks up to her; they're a little bit afraid of her. In awe, perhaps. This will devastate them and crush morale, which is at a real high. There is so much excitement about having all the redecorating finished. We have so many plans for increasing our involvement in Buxton tourism, the festivals, holding events here. It is meant to be a wonderful time for us. This could undermine all of that.'

'Oh, come on, they'd bounce back. It's a load of mobile phones and one stupid member of staff.' Joyce thought that was a little harsh of Ginger. Dennis could be viewed as somewhat melodramatic, but he was in shock himself.

'Maybe.' He stood up. 'Thank you both, but like you say, it's in my hands now and I need to make some decisions.'

'You're not going to call the police?' asked Ginger.

'Not yet. Can I ask that you don't either?'

'Of course, Dennis.' Joyce walked him to the door. 'You know where to find us if you need anything.'

Ginger walked over and gave him a hug. 'Sorry, my love, this is really hard. We'll support you whatever you do.'

He gave Ginger a kiss on the cheek and walked off down the corridor. Once the door was closed, Joyce went back to her seat.

'Ginger, you do realise this throws up a couple of other questions?'

'Such as?'

'We've always wondered if Caroline knew about the thefts, it was our first thought. Think about how much Mr Dalrymple wants to protect his wife. The lengths he's gone to, to ensure her actions remain hidden. What if Caroline found out and was going to report her to the police? That's the last thing Mr Dalrymple would have wanted.'

'Are you suggesting that he killed Caroline? He's an old man.'

'Agreed, but if he surprised her, then he might have had the strength to do it. He looks like he's always been fit and healthy, and people can tap into previously unused sources of physical strength once the adrenalin kicks in. And his determination to protect his wife would surely cause quite a flood of adrenalin should she be put at risk by the actions of another.'

'Well, if you're going to take that approach, then it puts Helen firmly back in our sights. She also had a lot to lose and Caroline could have worked out her role in the whole affair.'

'And Ed.' Joyce took over the flow of thoughts. 'I'm already of the opinion that he was selling that phone in order to protect his mother. Did he kill Caroline for the same reason?'

'You've already said that you don't think he did it,' Ginger reminded her. 'And what about the mysterious guest requesting a talk from Caroline? That suggests the killing was carefully planned, not a spur-of-the-moment thing.'

Joyce sighed. She was getting tired and her brain hurt.

'I know, I know. We've just created more questions than answers. I need some sleep. Tomorrow, we can continue following some of the other leads while Dennis decides what he's going to do about Mrs Dalrymple. Perhaps if he talks to Helen, she might let slip some information which points the finger of guilt at herself and the matter of Caroline's death will be resolved too.'

'We can only hope. Come on, girl. Time for bed. I'll wake you with coffee in the morning.' Ginger blew her a kiss, and then disappeared into her bedroom. Joyce watched her go, her final thoughts not about the dead woman, nor the thefts, but just how nice it must be to have someone who so firmly had your back, like Mr Dalrymple had his wife's. That no matter what happened, they were there for you.

Maybe one day, she thought as she turned off a table lamp and went to bed.

48

'*H*ave you decided what you're going to do?'

Dennis shook his head as he placed a full English breakfast in front of both Joyce and Ginger. Despite the stress of a difficult decision, he still looked immaculate and fresh-faced. Ginger knew it would have been out of character for Dennis to be anything else for long. He was committed to his role as the face of The Lodge; he viewed it as part of his job to look as smart as possible and appear very much in control, regardless of what else might be going on in his life.

'I spent hours talking it through with Tim last night. My head and my heart are currently debating it; I'll let you know who wins. Joyce, a full English? This doesn't seem very "you".'

'We're getting close to the end of our stay and I shall have to return to making my own breakfast soon. I decided to make the most of your hospitality and enjoy something that I would never make for myself.'

'As you should, my dear. If you would like anything else – a few more rashers of bacon or an extra round of toast – do let me know.'

'What's going on with him?' Ginger had watched Graham

Bennett stick his head through the door to the dining room; he hadn't looked happy. He was walking away as Dennis turned.

'He's been in a funny mood all week, and now he's started pestering me for more work. Once the jobs are done upstairs, that's everything finished for a long time, I hope. There'll be the usual wear and tear, and I'm sure I'll need him for the odd repair here and there, but nothing significant.'

'You'd think he was hard up for cash,' said Joyce, looking thoughtful. 'I thought you said his business had gone from strength to strength and he was doing really well. When did things really change for the better for him, can you recall?'

Dennis put the coffee pot down on the table, but held on to it while he thought.

'Around the time we started the work upstairs. I was lucky to get him; his schedule exploded a couple of weeks after he came here. We'd used him in the past for jobs as and when they arose, but this was a major project. I think he'd started to receive the payments for a couple of big jobs he'd done just before this one and he was able to bring some lads on board. They did a lot of the "heavy lifting"; he did the more ornate design-inspired work, and then he was out preparing for some future contracts. He also got the job with John Bradbury.'

'Was that a recent thing as well?' Joyce asked.

'Yes. He was awarded the contract about two months ago.'

Joyce and Ginger looked at one another and smiled.

'What? What are you two not telling me? Ginger Salt, we've never kept secrets from one another, don't start now.' Dennis pulled up a chair and sat down. 'Come on, ladies, don't tease a chap.'

'It's very simple really,' said Ginger. 'I'm surprised you haven't worked it out for yourself.' She took a painfully slow sip of her coffee before letting out a long, 'Aaaah. Very nice.'

'Ginger Salt, you're a pain in the…'

'What am I, Dennis? I didn't quite catch that.'

'A thing of beauty, my dear. But if you ever want to drink in my bar again...'

'Alright, alright. Graham Bennett starts working for you on the renovation about four months ago. He's well known and respected locally, but he's largely a one-man band. Within a matter of weeks, he has apparently received significant payment for some previous work – such a large payment, he's able to afford a couple of lads to help him out while he does other things. He gets a new car and overall becomes a man with cash to spare, leading the life of a boss who can enjoy his success while his team does a lot of the heavy lifting. He also gets a big contract to work for John Bradbury. So far, so good?'

'Correct,' Dennis confirmed. Ginger looked at Joyce, who took over.

'Now, all of a sudden, our Mr Bennett is back to work. The smart shirts have been exchanged for well-worn t-shirts. He's given the team he employed the marching orders and he's turning up in the company van rather than his fancy car. Now, Mr General Manager, think of the timing of all of this.'

'Have you two never heard of getting to the point?'

'All in good time. Ginger and I should be allowed to enjoy ourselves, having worked it out.

'Alright. Graham starts work here at The Lodge. He recognises John Bradbury. Their paths are bound to have crossed in the building trade, so he knows that John is married and not to a woman called Lydia. It's a small world; he might have seen John's wife at an industry dinner or just in passing. Graham realises John is having an affair with Lydia, but unlike you and your staff, he has little sense of discretion. He starts blackmailing John. Hence the arrival of men he can now afford to employ to help him out so he can go and enjoy life.

'I doubt he was actually scouting for more work; he was out buying a new car and heaven knows what else. It seems money runs through his fingers like water. Part of that blackmail included being given the job on John's new building project. To explain the money he had all of a sudden, he lied about a few contracts, including claiming that he had been given a contract at Charleton House. I checked; he hasn't.

'However, it all fell apart recently, when John got divorce papers from his wife. As his affair is no longer secret, he can no longer be blackmailed. That's why we saw him arguing with Graham; I guess he'd given Graham his marching orders. And now... well, Graham's spent most of the money he got from John and the source has dried up. He has had to let his team go, he's back to work himself and he's begging you for more business. Karma has made a visit and bitten him in the derrière.'

'Well, I'm glad he's pretty much finished the job here if he's going to be dragged off to prison for extortion. Will you contact the police or should I?'

'We'll do it,' Ginger said quickly. 'We could do with keeping DS Harnby sweet. She doesn't seem to have worked out that we withheld evidence from her. If we give her some good news – well, not exactly good news, but you know what I mean – maybe she'll turn a blind eye to anything she does find out about us.'

'Can I ask you leave it a couple of hours?'

'Why?'

'I could do with Graham finishing the work upstairs. He hasn't got much to do and he's not showing signs of doing a runner.'

'Lunchtime,' Joyce said. Ginger let out a little groan. A woman sitting a couple of tables away heard and looked up.

'Sorry,' Ginger said, looking at her. 'It was the sausages, I'd steer clear.'

'Oi!' Dennis swung round in his seat to face the shocked-looking guest. 'There's nothing wrong with the sausages, she's jesting. And scaring my guests,' he added once he had turned back to the table. 'What are you doing? What's wrong?'

'We've just added another name to the list of potential killers, and they're all still *potential*. If Caroline found out what Graham was up to, then he also had reason to get rid of her. If she had blabbed, then he would have lost a lot of money. There will have been so many opportunities for Caroline to overhear a conversation, or maybe she just put the pieces together like we did.'

'So we have John thinking that Caroline might reveal the affair, and she's trying to prevent him getting his hands on Morton Hall in order to develop it and make a fortune; we have Mr Dalrymple who – if he'd found the strength – could have been protecting his wife; and we have Graham who was blackmailing John, and Caroline could have lost him that source of income. Then you might want to add Helen and Ed to that list, but I'm not convinced Ed has it in him.'

'And Helen wouldn't do it,' Dennis quickly added. 'She might be a thief, but she's not a killer. She looks at you like she'd happily strangle you when she's annoyed, but she's not actually capable of it.'

'We'll take your word for that,' said Ginger as she watched a lost-looking man who had just walked into the dining room. He spotted Dennis and walked over.

'Mr Matty?'

Dennis stood up. 'That's me. How can I help you, sir?'

'Reception sent me in here to find you. I have some things for a Joyce Brocklehurst and I'm told you'd know where to find her.'

Before Dennis had a chance to reply, Joyce stood up.

'I am she. A pleasure to meet you, how can I be of assistance?'

Ginger recognised the slight purr in Joyce's voice; the man was reasonably good-looking.

'Well, as you've found the lovely Ms Brocklehurst, I will leave you all to it.' Dennis nodded to the newcomer, smiled at the two women, and then walked towards the door.

'To what do we owe this pleasure?' Joyce asked as she indicated a chair to the visitor.

'I'm Jim, Frank Flagg's son. Frank from The Cedars. He asked me to drop some paintings off, something about an ex-student of his.' As he spoke, the man pulled a number of sheets of stiff paper out of a plastic bag and put them on the table.

The colour drained from both the women's faces. Ginger glanced up to check that Dennis was nowhere near their table. He'd left the room entirely, which helped her relax, a little.

The pictures Jim had laid out were a mixture of paint, newspaper cuttings and photographs. Nature played a strong part: a background of trees painted in watercolour was overlaid with images of local scenery. They were a little crude, but the artworks showed real potential and it was easy to see why Frank had been impressed and had kept them.

But Ginger couldn't focus on how impressive the work was. She turned to look at the wall nearest to them. The painting hanging there was also mixed media. Grainy black-and-white photos of the Pavilion Gardens being enjoyed by Edwardian ladies, newspaper clippings and watercolour paintings had been meshed together in a beautiful collage.

There was no escaping the fact that Frank's student had been Tim Starling. Tim Starling, who would likely have been very, very angry at Dorothy Clatworthy for splitting his family up and taking him from all that was familiar, even though her intention had been to protect him. Tim Starling, who had a strong reason to want revenge.

49

'Does your father mind if we borrow these?' Joyce asked. 'Not at all. He said to leave them with you and you can return them when you visit him so he can thrash you at Scrabble again.' Jim Flagg smiled, looking a little apologetic for the message.

'Thank you, I will.' Joyce hurriedly put them back in the bag; she didn't want Dennis to see them. 'We need to go, but I'm sure you'd be welcome to stay and have a coffee.'

'Thank you, but I can't.'

Joyce and Ginger walked Jim to the front door of The Lodge and said goodbye before scurrying back to their room. With the door firmly shut, Ginger fell back against it.

'Bloody hell, what do we do now? It was Tim! Tim's family was pulled apart by Caroline's mother. Do you think this was why he suggested she get a job here? So he knew where she was while he planned his revenge? This is going to break Dennis's heart, he adores Tim and he's been so happy these last few years. Everything has been coming together here at The Lodge, he and Tim have settled down. How do I break this to him? What do we do now?'

'Well, first of all, you're going to come over here. The door doesn't need your help staying upright and anyone walking past can hear every word. Sit down, woman!'

While Ginger moved to the sofa, Joyce started to pace. John, Graham, Mr Dalrymple, now Tim. The list was growing longer, but this one was the murkiest possibility of all. It potentially had someone taking the blame for the destruction of a family, years of festering anger and a desire for revenge; not necessarily on the cause of the anger, Dorothy Clatworthy, but a chance to harm her family just as she had harmed his, or so he might well have believed. Of course, Dorothy had done no such thing; she was doing her job, and as far as Joyce could tell she did the right thing, but it would come as no surprise to her if Tim saw things differently. He'd been a child back then; there was no guarantee he was going to view things rationally.

'Alright,' said Ginger, 'but you need to sit down, too, you're putting me on edge.'

Joyce did as she was told and crossed one long leg over the other, resting each arm on an armrest. She never slouched and Ginger often accused her of looking like a Bond villain, an image she rather liked.

'Can you remember what Tim said about his movements that day?' Joyce asked.

'He'd gone to the Sheffield Art Gallery; he wanted to see the Anish Kapoor exhibition. He had the train ticket, and it was a Saturday so we know it was definitely open. And he'd shown Harnby the train ticket.'

'They don't always stamp the train tickets, though, and if he changed at Stockport, he won't have had to go through any barriers. He could have bought the tickets and never got on the train; the fact that he still has them or that they are spotless wouldn't prove or disprove that. The police would have checked that the exhibition was open, though, and that he had a ticket for it.'

'True, but he could have booked online and never actually

used it.' Ginger looked as if she was thinking so hard, her head was about to explode. 'I wish I had a cigarette.'

Joyce was horrified. 'You don't smoke. I've never seen you smoke.'

'No, but this feels like a cigarette-worthy moment and it's too early for alcohol.'

Joyce agreed; about the drinking, anyway. It was always five o'clock somewhere. But morning gin-drinking wasn't going to help.

Joyce laid out her plan for the day. 'We need to speak to Tim. We should at least give him a chance to explain himself before we say anything to Dennis, so we need to find out when he's next coming by The Lodge. If it's not for a while, then we'll have to call him and arrange to meet.

'Then I think we should go and talk to John. I don't care how bad-tempered he is, I want to find out about him and Caroline. He had a lot of reasons to want her out of the way and I still feel like he's our number-one suspect. Or he was until I saw those paintings. Ready?' There was no response from Ginger. 'Ready?'

'Yes, I'm ready; I was just thinking. If Tim is behind this, there isn't going to be any trial. I'm going to rip him limb from limb. If a couple of things had been different, I'd probably have married Dennis, and I've always said if someone hurt him, they'd have me to answer to.' She looked as though she was getting herself all riled up before entering a boxing ring.

'Alright, well, can you just hold off until we get all the evidence we need to take to Harnby? If you do kill him, I want to make sure we've got plenty of proof that you were driven to it and we can put in a plea of insanity.'

'They'd have to bloody catch me first.'

'Okay, can you plan all that later, please? We've got places to be and you're driving. The last thing I want is you getting behind the wheel while you're in a murderous mood. I'm keen to solve this, but not keen enough to lose my life in the process.'

Joyce tossed Ginger the car keys, which promptly disappeared down the side of the sofa and led to Ginger burrowing behind the cushions with her bum in the air. Joyce considered making a joke about barrage balloons, but decided that Ginger might turn on her and she wasn't convinced she could fight her off when she was in this kind of mood.

It was another ten minutes before they were ready to go, which gave Joyce time to phone John's office and make an inno-cent-sounding enquiry about his whereabouts to the receptionist. He was going to be back at the building site, so they didn't have far to go. As they left, Joyce sent Ginger on ahead to the car and stuck her head into Dennis's office.

'We're off out. Is Tim coming round later? Thought we should all have a drink, maybe dinner. You'll be a bit busy tomorrow with the celebrations.'

'Definitely, he'd like that. He's coming by this afternoon and I'll tell him.'

'We'll be back by then, so I'll be able to catch him myself. See you later.'

'TTFN. Try and stay out of trouble.'

'With Ginger by my side?'

Dennis laughed.

---

50

*G*inger had lived her whole life in Derbyshire. She was used to the villages and hills, venturing into cities only when she had to for work, or the occasional treat: the theatre or to do some Christmas shopping. Buxton wasn't a city, but it was a reasonable-sized town, so she was starting to feel fidgety. They had spent too much time sniffing around the darker side of humankind and she needed to stride out across some fields, arms wide, skirts billowing and occasionally singing into the wind at full volume just for the sheer hell of it. But at least Buxton was pretty and its Georgian architecture was fine; for that she was grateful.

The building site wasn't very pretty, though, and Ginger had a hard time imagining that it ever would be. It didn't matter how bespoke John Bradbury made each house, they would still be boxes to her. Plain, poorly built modern boxes that had little charm and would probably all start springing leaks within twelve months. Ginger loved her stone cottage, with its beds of lavender, geraniums, pinks and peonies. More than 300 years old and it still hadn't needed any significant work; just cosmetic alterations when she wanted to put her stamp on it. The plumbing had needed upgrading to the 20th century and the toilet moving inside, but that was before she arrived. It was as solid as… well, the Derbyshire stone it was made out of.

As Ginger steered around clay coloured puddles that looked large enough to swallow the car, she wondered what sort of a welcome they were going to get and decided she would leave the keys in the ignition just in case they needed to make a fast getaway.

'So, how are we doing this?' she asked Joyce as she stepped out of the car.

'Same as before. We're just trying to find out more about how our sweet, sweet niece died.' Joyce looked at her with sad eyes; at least, Ginger assumed that was her aim. It made her look like she'd had too much to drink and was about to fall asleep.

'What?' Joyce asked. 'You're looking at me funny.'

'Don't do that, don't pull that sad face. At best, he'll offer you a seat and a glass of water, and possibly a leaflet for Alcoholics Anonymous.'

Joyce pulled another face and wrapped her pale-pink cashmere scarf around her neck with such gusto, Ginger was concerned that she might strangle herself. Joyce tugged her skirt down into position, bent the wing mirror up and took a quick look. She appeared satisfied with what she saw.

Joyce's shoes were completely unsuitable for a building site: 4-inch heels that she was trying to prevent from sinking into the mixture of sand and mud by tottering along on her tiptoes, and she was rather good at it. As they stood outside the door to John's office, Joyce whipped out a tissue from her bag and gave her shoes a quick clean. She followed it up with a firm knock on the door. Ginger watched every step of the process with amusement.

'YES.' It was a shout without much of an invitation behind it. 'Oh, hello.' John stood as they entered. 'Can I help? Hang on, you were here before. What do you want?' He clearly wasn't happy to see them, but he wasn't quite as angry as last time; at least he wasn't kicking them out.

'We just want to talk,' Ginger said. 'Can we take a seat?'

John took a quick look at his watch, and then sat down. 'Sure.' He did seem calmer than last time, but that wasn't quite the right description; there was something else there, too. He didn't have the same kind of energy. If they angered him, Ginger wasn't sure they'd be thrown out with quite such fury. Shown the door, yes, but this felt different, although she knew it didn't guarantee a calm conversation that would result in him admitting to the murder of Caroline. The best they could hope for was that he would make a mistake; say something that didn't add up, something that incriminated him and might lead to further evidence.

'You know why we're here.' There was no threat in Joyce's voice. 'We just want to find out more about our niece and we think you can help us. What can you tell us about Morton Hall?'

John looked a little surprised, but not defensive. 'I'm hoping to buy it, turn it into flats and a community centre, amongst other things. Why on earth do you want to know about that?'

'We're aware that Caroline didn't want you to buy it, she was fighting any plans to convert the building. Did you see her at the meetings? Talk to her? You must have had a lot to argue about.'

John appeared to be deep in thought. Ginger imagined him desperately running through excuses, trying to remember if there had been witnesses to any arguments he had had with Caroline.

'We talked, yes, often.'

'So you did have contact outside The Lodge?'

'On a regular basis, yes.'

'Was she very vociferous in her fight against your purchase?'

'Her fight against... what fight? I don't understand. Where are you getting this from?'

Ginger decided to step in. 'We've read her notes: all the research she did on the building, its history, its value. She was clearly determined that it would be preserved and was keen to fight off anyone who would do any damage to it. She'd spent a great deal of time on this, it meant a lot to her.'

A smile spread slowly across John's face. It wasn't a smile of triumph; he was remembering something.

'It did. It meant a great deal to her, ladies, but I'm afraid you've got the wrong end of the stick. Caroline was indeed very passionate about saving Morton Hall, but she was also extremely pragmatic and knew that money needed to be spent on it and that a new use would need to be found for it. There is one developer trying to buy the land who plans on tearing the building down and putting a new block of flats and shops in its place. But that's not me. Caroline and I were working together.

'As you say, she had done a great deal of research, which I was going to use to ensure we preserved as much of the original design as possible. Caroline's work went into my planning application, to illustrate how sympathetic my project would be. Yes, I want to turn it into flats on the upper floors, but there will be a space for the community to use on the ground floor, and the building will be handled very carefully. I can show you copies of all the documents if you'd like.'

He reached for a folder on a shelf behind him, but Joyce stopped him.

'So you got on with her?'

'Very well, yes.'

'You didn't argue with her at The Lodge?'

He smiled. 'In the early days, yes, she made the same assumptions as you: that I wanted to tear the building down. It was a while before I had the chance to sit her down, at which point we realised that we could work together on it.'

So Lydia had got the wrong end of the stick when she told Joyce that Caroline had disapproved of her and John's affair. She *had* seen them arguing, and of course John would be annoyed with someone trying to scupper his plans. If John didn't talk about his work much – and let's face it, if he was having a fun-filled naughty getaway in a hotel, his mind was hardly likely to be on his work – then it wasn't surprising Lydia had misunderstood.

'So you didn't argue with her because she was making snide comments about extramarital affairs?' Ginger bit her lip; she hadn't meant to say that out loud. There was a momentary flicker of anger in his eyes, but it vanished as quickly as it had arrived. He shook his head, his finger tracing the pattern on a lump of stone that sat on his desk.

'What is that?' Joyce angled her head around to try to see the other side. John turned it so they could both see. There was a pattern of a flower moulded into it.

'Caroline had this made. There used to be a line of similar stones above the doorway of Morton Hall. Most were crumbling and they were all in a pretty bad way. Caroline found another building with the exact same design in perfect condition, so she had a mould made. We were going to recreate them. She gave me this as a gift; I use it as a paperweight.'

He turned it back around and continued to trace the line of the flower with his finger. After a few moments, Joyce broke the awkward silence.

'We know about Graham.'

'What about him?'

'That he was blackmailing you. I guess you're looking for another carpenter now?'

John laughed. 'The man's an idiot. At worst an annoyance. I simply didn't need his services.'

'But he was blackmailing you?'

'He thought he was.'

'What do you mean? He was or he wasn't.'

John waved his hand in the air as if he was half-heartedly swatting a fly.

'Yes, he was. I'm sure that to him, it was a lot of money, although he certainly spent it quick enough, but it was spare change to me. I really didn't want him working on the houses up here; that was frustrating and I needed to find a way out of that. But I had time to figure something out. He was bound to do or say something that meant I could throw it all back at him. I would have found a way out of it before long.'

'Not that you needed to in the end. The solution presented itself, didn't it? Your wife filed for divorce so he could no longer blackmail you.'

Joyce looked at the pile of papers on the corner of the desk as she spoke. So did John.

'How did you know about that?'

'The solicitors' firm. I used the same company for my last divorce so I know what they specialise in. I just hope for your sake that your wife isn't using Grantham Macintosh, he's very good.'

He laughed. 'Ah, I better watch out then.'

Ginger couldn't help but notice that he didn't seem too angry. He was free of Graham; he and Lydia could move on; he didn't have to sneak around anymore. It was easy to understand why there was a calmness to him. A lot had resolved itself.

'Now, ladies, unless there's anything else, I really ought to get on and earn some money.' He smiled weakly at Joyce. 'Especially if what you say about Macintosh is true.'

51

'What do you think?' Ginger asked as she drove them back to the hotel. 'Do you think he killed her?'

'No, I don't. But something isn't right. We've seen all sorts of emotions from that man; I just don't quite understand what they all mean.'

'Well, things are about to get much more emotional and possibly very unpleasant.'

'Why?'

'We're going to talk to Tim. Or, should I say Thomas?'

The Lodge reception was busy when Ginger and Joyce returned. A stream of workmen were leaving with pots of paint and toolboxes under their arms. Housekeeping staff passed them in the opposite direction, trying to get a head start on preparing the new rooms for the following day. Joyce pressed herself against the reception desk as a workman in white overalls strode past with a ladder under his arm.

'Sorry, Miss,' he called over his shoulder.

'Did he get paint on your skirt?' asked Barbara from behind reception.

'He called me Miss, so he can get anything he wants on my skirt.'

Helen walked past, issuing instructions on her mobile phone as she climbed the stairs. It seemed that Dennis had yet to come to a decision, or his decision had been one of leniency.

'Shall we get some lunch?' Ginger asked. 'We have some time to kill until Tim gets here and we may as well spend it eating.'

Joyce nodded, a small knot forming in her stomach as she followed Ginger into the dining room. She felt as if they were about to rip apart another family. She'd never met Tim before this week, but Ginger's affection for him had been contagious and she had yet to see anything about the man she didn't like.

She ordered a glass of water, ignoring the questioning look from Ginger; she wanted to keep a clear head. The leek and potato soup, which she knew under normal conditions would be delicious and warming, now tasted bland, the cubes of potato hard to swallow. This was no reflection on the chef but rather her state of mind. It had all seemed rather jolly at the start of the week: enjoying the services of a very nice boutique hotel while the weather outside struggled with the last wet and grey throes of winter, and all the while she and Ginger could play Agatha Christie. Caroline's body hadn't been found in the library – the library that the hotel didn't even have – but that was all the week needed. That and an irritating detective with an oily moustache, which Detective Sergeant Harnby could hardly provide.

Joyce tried hard to ensure that she wasn't prone to fits of emotion, at least not outwardly. She had a reputation to maintain, after all, but Caroline had seemed to fade into the background as the focus had been on other people's desires, habits and greed, and that didn't sit comfortably with her. If Caroline had become the target of Tim's anger, an act of revenge for something she'd had nothing to do with, then Joyce couldn't be sure she wouldn't join Ginger in taking matters into her own hands.

She kept hold of that thought for a moment, gradually letting go of the image of the warm, genial artist she had enjoyed drinks with. That made the thought of the forthcoming confrontation easier. If she could just keep a lid on those darker feelings, then she'd be ready for the conversation they were about to have.

After picking at a miniature carrot cake – and miniature meant you could have fitted it in a matchbox – Joyce scrolled aimlessly through various websites on her phone. Ginger had picked up a copy of *Derbyshire Life* and was reading about dry-stone walling.

'I really ought to go on one of these courses, make a proper job of the wall at the back of my house.'

Joyce was only half listening, until her thoughts were interrupted by laughter. She hadn't seen Mr and Mrs Dalrymple take a seat in the dining room, but they had been joined by Tim who now patted Mr Dalrymple on the shoulder as they shared a joke. Then he walked away from their table, straight towards Joyce and Ginger.

'Hello, hello, hello. Enjoy your lunch?' He looked at the crumbs on Joyce's plate. 'Carrot cake?' He shook his head. 'Give me a honking great slice of moist carrot cake, big enough to be used as a door wedge. I can't stand these fancy little excuses, hardly big enough to transfer the slightest hint of flavour. I shouldn't say that, of course, but Dennis knows. On one occasion, he fetched me twenty at once and piled them into the shape of a cake wedge. He got brownie points for that.'

He reached for a chair from an empty table and sat down. 'Dennis said you were looking for me. How can I help?'

'We were hoping you'd have time for a chat. Are you busy?' Ginger asked.

'I have to finish hanging a couple of pictures upstairs, but it won't take long and can wait. So is now good?'

Joyce nodded at Ginger.

'Great,' she said. 'Maybe we should go to our room.'

'Oh, OK.'

Tim looked confused, and then concerned. Joyce avoided any eye contact as she gathered her coat and bag and led the way to the Stanage Suite.

52

The cleaners had already paid a visit to Joyce and Ginger's suite. If it wasn't for the magazines on the table and Ginger's knitting on the armchair, it would have looked as if they had just checked in. Fresh flowers were on the coffee table: the bonus of being friends with the boss, no doubt, or the action of a nervous head of housekeeping? Ginger assumed that Helen was still unaware that her little sideline had been discovered.

Tim wandered in with his hands in his pockets.

'Nice room. This is where we put some friends of mine when they visited before Christmas.' He sounded calm enough, but it felt like awkward small talk. Ginger felt sick and she was sure her temperature was rising. This was excruciating.

'Have a seat,' Joyce offered. They all found somewhere to sit – something to do in the uncomfortable silence. Then Ginger opted to speak before she ran out of the room in a crazed attempt to avoid one of the most uncomfortable conversations of her life.

'Tim, this is really difficult, but there's something we need to talk to you about, and I don't know if Dennis knows.'

'Go on.'

'Tell us about your relationship with Dorothy Clatworthy.'

'Who?'

'Caroline's mother, Dorothy. Mrs Clatworthy. She was head-mistress at St John's.'

For a moment, his eyes remained neutral. There was no sign of panic; he simply looked curious, as though he was hoping they would give him a clue as to what they were talking about. Joyce, who had opted for the armchair, was again sitting straight-backed and legs crossed. Her expression was also one of curios-ity, that and concern.

'I know she died a couple of years ago, but I never met her.'

'But you went to her school. You must have run into her at one time or another, been hauled up in front of her for running in the corridor or skipping class?' Ginger was hoping that he would eventually open up and she wouldn't have to accuse him directly.

After an uncomfortable pause, he ran his fingers through his hair, and then spoke.

'Oh yeah, I remember,' he said, seemingly surprised. 'God, that was years ago. She looked terrifying, but she was alright really.'

'Did Caroline know?'

'Doubt it. We didn't talk about it, and I'm a bit younger than she was. There's no reason for her to have known.'

'There's also the matter of your name,' Joyce said. Tim laughed awkwardly.

'What do you mean, my name?'

'Thomas Stafford. If she had remembered you, Caroline would have known you as Thomas Stafford.'

He held the look of confusion briefly, before appearing to give up.

'How did you find out?'

'Teachers. What happened to your family was clearly very sad, and also very memorable.'

'And we were shown this,' Ginger added as she got up. From

the drawer in the desk, she retrieved the pictures that Jim had delivered. She laid them out on the coffee table.

'Where did you get those from?' This time, Tim sounded genuinely surprised.

'Your old art teacher held on to them; he knew you had real talent.'

Tim's face glowed. It was moving that someone who had gone through so much had managed to make a success of his life, but they were here because he might have destroyed someone else's life, and his own.

Ginger took a deep breath, girded her proverbial loins and spoke.

'Tim, your family was pulled apart because Dorothy Clatworthy made a call to social services. You have a very good, and understandable, reason to hate her, to want revenge.'

Tim looked up from the artwork.

'What do you mean, revenge?'

'I'm sure it was a truly horrible, horrible time. You've had many years to think about it. Then when you ran into Caroline in London, you had the chance to get her up here, and you'd know exactly where she was while you decided what to do.'

Tim looked at Ginger, then Joyce.

'Do you think... do you really think I killed... Are you out of your mind? Ginger, come on, you know me.'

'I thought I did, but you're not even called Tim. What else have you kept hidden?'

'I went to the art gallery in Sheffield. The police have seen my rail tickets; I'm sure they checked out my story.'

It was Joyce's turn. 'We all know the guards don't always stamp rail tickets. You could have bought those, but never used them. I looked at the gallery website. The exhibition you went to was indeed on, but when I phoned the gallery, they said they'd had to close it for one day because a pipe had burst. That day was last Saturday. If you become a significant suspect, then I have no doubt that after further investigation, the police will find more holes in your alibi.'

'Have you told Dennis any of this?' he asked. Ginger shook her head slowly.

'Not a thing. I don't plan on breaking his heart without checking out all the evidence.'

Tim slumped forward with his head in his hands for a few moments, before sitting back up.

'I didn't kill Caroline. I barely knew her. Meeting her in London was sheer coincidence, and when I told her about The Lodge, it was just a suggestion. It didn't become part of some grand plot to kill the woman.

'When we were put into care, I was angry. As angry as any teenager would be. I felt like Mrs Clatworthy had destroyed my world. My mum tried hard, she really did, but she just couldn't cope. At the time, I couldn't see beyond my own anger, the unfairness of it all. I was a kid. But I haven't harboured a lifelong desire for revenge. The thing is, if Mrs Clatworthy hadn't called social services, if I hadn't been moved into foster care, I might not be where I am now. My mum didn't know one end of a paintbrush from the other, but the family I was placed with loved art. They took me to art galleries, paid for classes and encouraged me. That was why I went to art school.'

He picked up a painting from the coffee table. 'I still can't believe Frank kept these, but they might have been the entire body of my work if things had stayed as they were, and I'd have been... I don't know what, but it wouldn't have been pretty, I'm sure. I didn't hate Mrs Clatworthy. Well, I did, but I got over it. If anything, I owe the life I have right now to her. She rescued me.'

'Why the name change?' asked Ginger.

'Starling was my mum's maiden name. My dad was a waste of space and I wanted to remove any connection to him. My mum died when I was twenty-one and I wanted to honour her in some way. I'd already taken to calling myself Tim; I wanted to distance myself from my past.'

'Does Dennis know any of this?'

He shook his head. 'Only that my first name is actually Thomas, but not why I stopped using that. The rest isn't something I talk about, I'm used to pretending it never happened. Then as time went on, it seemed a bit late to mention it.'

'Why the lies about where you were the day Caroline died?'

'I knew as soon as I found out that Caroline had been killed that my past could make me a suspect. I didn't have a good alibi, so I lied about the gallery and hoped that no one found out.'

Ginger looked at the tired man before her. The more he explained, the more she saw the boy he had been, angry and pushed around by adults who controlled his life. And then the adult he had become came to the fore: sensible, forgiving. As much as his mum had struggled, she'd given him the foundations, the character to build on.

Tim looked at more of the artwork.

'I still can't believe he kept these,' he repeated.

'You should go and see him,' Joyce said. 'He's a nice old chap, very fond of you.'

'I will, I'd like to see him.'

They let him sit with his thoughts for a while, until he broke the silence.

'I should talk to Dennis now. I don't want to have this hanging over me and I've kept him in the dark for too long.' He stood up slowly, but with a single smooth movement. Ginger envied the lack of stiffness in his joints. She gathered all the paintings and put them in the bag before handing them to him.

'Joyce will tell you how to contact Frank later.'

Tim walked slowly to the door, pausing briefly to thank them both, and then let himself out. Neither Joyce nor Ginger said a word. Ginger firmly believed that he'd had nothing to do with Caroline's death, and she could see that Joyce agreed. That was the good news. The bad news: Caroline's killer was still out there.

53

There was no sign of Dennis or Tim when Joyce and Ginger made their way to the bar later that evening. Lisa told them that Dennis had taken the evening off and they both decided it was a good sign that he was going to spend quality time with Tim. Regardless of how well the difficult conversation went, they would at least have a whole evening to focus on one another and not be distracted by the various shenanigans of hotel guests or last-minute concerns about tomorrow's party.

Joyce ordered a glass of champagne, Ginger an Old Fashioned.

'We're going to have one hell of a bar tab,' Ginger pointed out.

'Why's that?'

'The deal was if we worked out who the killer was by Friday, Dennis would cover the bill; if we didn't, it was ours to pay.'

Joyce tried to run through everything they'd drunk since arriving Saturday lunchtime. It was painful, but not the first eye-watering bar bill she'd ever been handed.

'True, but we will have worked out one thing.'

'What's that?' Ginger looked baffled.

'We might not have worked out who killed Caroline, but we have confirmed we can go away together and not want to kill one another.'

'I'll toast to that. So, where to next? I've always fancied exploring the Yorkshire coast.'

Joyce curled a lip. She had a very long list to draw upon.

'Bugger that, I'm thinking Paris, or Budapest.'

'We have everything we need on our own fair shores.'

'I take it all back,' Joyce said. 'I'm not going anywhere with you again. You'll be taking me to a knitting needle factory or showing me the smallest house in England.'

'No, but the Kendal Pencil Museum is actually quite enjoyable.'

'That's the Lake District, not Yorkshire.'

'Pedant. I don't see what you're complaining about. I brought you to stay in a hotel thirty minutes from your front door and we've had murder, theft, passion, heartbreak, family drama, art, history, a broken marriage. You've thrown yourself down a zip line, eaten fabulous food, drunk far too much alcohol and had more outfit changes than the cast of a West End musical. All we need is some jealousy, missing millions and an illegitimate child and we can settle down in a care home with Frank, having experienced all that life can throw at us.'

Joyce was a little surprised by the list. Toss in a very good massage and not having to make her own bed for a week and it was almost perfect as breaks went.

'I'll admit, this week has been far more interesting than I was expecting. For a start, I wasn't expecting it to be a week.'

'I hope that wasn't the high point. And it's not over. We have a party tomorrow night and Dennis throws fabulous parties. You've all night tonight and tomorrow morning to decide what to wear. We should both go back to the spa and have a…'

'Hang on just one moment there. You want to return to the spa? Do you mean to tell me that you've been won over and you'll actually try something a little more adventurous?' If this was all that she'd achieved this week, then Joyce would take it. It was a promising sign for any future trips the two women made together. If Ginger could be truly won over, then maybe a weekend in a spa resort might be on the cards.

'I'll admit, I did rather enjoy the facial. I might be prepared to have a go at a massage.'

'Well, I never. Lisa, another round please. We have something to celebrate.'

With full glasses in hand, they toasted the art of pampering. Once they'd finished, they sat quietly for a few minutes until a couple of familiar faces entered the room.

'We can be sure that Dennis hasn't come to a decision about the thefts.' Ginger pointed with her glass to a sofa where Mr and Mrs Dalrymple had taken a seat. Mrs Dalrymple looked as happy as ever, saying hello to a couple sitting at a table close by. Mr Dalrymple placed an order with a server who had gone over to them.

'Maybe he wants to get the party out of the way, give them the chance for a last hurrah.'

'I wonder how Graham is doing with DS Harnby?'

Joyce had forgotten about him. 'Do you think she might actually have the killer in a cell as we speak?' It was a good point, and brought with it another benefit. Joyce enjoyed a mouthful of champagne before saying, 'Well, if she has, we might be able to get away without paying the bar bill. We phoned Harnby because we knew Graham was blackmailing John, so Dennis might argue the point, but we did consider the possibility that he might have killed Caroline to keep her quiet.'

'And him? Mr Dalrymple?'

Joyce wasn't sure. It didn't feel right. His love for his wife meant he would try to do anything to protect her and her reputation. For it to lead him to kill was a stretch; not impossible, but a stretch all the same.

She watched as Helen walked through the room. She was in her coat and had likely finished her shift for the night. Helen caught Joyce's eye and her walk slowed; it was barely noticeable, but seeing Joyce and Ginger had certainly given her a momentary jolt and she'd looked very briefly nervous. Then she smiled at someone out of Joyce's sight.

Helen could be about to lose her job and maybe she knew it. Perhaps there was more going on than just getting rid of stolen goods, and she thought Joyce and Ginger were onto her. The hardness that Dennis had said was only superficial was clear on her features and Joyce was convinced it ran a lot deeper than that.

She stared into her champagne glass. They'd failed to work out who'd killed Caroline and it was nearly Friday. What had started as a bit of a lark had actually turned into something that meant a great deal to her, and the most important part was that she had been working side by side with Ginger. She watched her friend as Ginger showed Lisa how to turn a piece of orange peel into a beautiful flower-shaped garnish for her glass. Ginger had been right: adventure was possible right outside her own door.

Joyce woke up and looked at the alarm clock: 23.42. She tossed and turned a few times; her back was sore and she couldn't get comfortable.

She was pleased that Ginger had suggested another trip to the spa and thought about what treatments she would opt for. Another massage was definite, perhaps hot rocks, and if a manicurist was on site, she'd have her nails done for the party. It would be a nice treat before she returned to work on Monday, and Lydia's treatment room was calm and relaxing. The soft and fluffy towels; the peach-coloured walls; even the fire exit was tucked away in the corner and didn't stand out like the ugly safety necessity it was. It would be good to be able to relax there without having to quiz the poor woman about a murder victim.

Joyce sat bolt upright. The fire exit!

'GINGER!' she shouted. Her bedroom door was closed and no doubt Ginger's was too. She threw off the bedclothes and ran into Ginger's room, pulling the sheets off her groaning friend.

'Whaaaaat?'

'Text Dennis quick. I know who killed Caroline, and if you send the text before midnight, he pays the bar bill.'

ennis was waiting for them when they went down to breakfast. He looked at his watch.

'Heavens, we've only just shielded our eyes from the crack of dawn. Could you two not sleep, or have you had enough beauty sleep and you're afraid of undermining the confidence of all the other women at the hotel? Or is it because you've figured out a way to avoid paying your bar tab? Thanks for that, by the way, Ginger; I'd only just got off to sleep when your message arrived. Of course, I didn't get a drop of sleep after that. So…'

'Coffee, one avocado toast with poached eggs, and I'll have a bacon butty.' Ginger laid out their breakfast demands.

'We don't do bacon butties.'

'Okay, delicate crust-less sandwiches using bacon made from hand-rendered artisanal pig which has been fed on blueberry soup and asparagus pâté, had Shakespeare read to it every night, listened to opera and sacrificed its life in a special ceremony. After being prepared by a team of virgins, its bacon is served on brioche bread that you made yourself overnight and will be brought to me on a silver platter.'

Dennis was as posh as Ginger behind the tailored suits, i.e.

not at all, so he could get her a bacon butty, regardless of how he described it on his fancy menus. She was hungry.

'I only use pigs fed on cranberry soup, but yes, we can do that for you. And then you're going to tell me what's going on.'

'Of course, dear, and add a couple of glasses of orange juice,' she called as he disappeared into the kitchen.

'He seems alright,' Joyce observed. 'So can we safely assume that the conversation with Tim went okay?'

'He's well-practised at putting on a façade for the guests, but I'm not getting any of the stressed or upset vibes I can usually detect when he's not himself. I think that we can indeed assume that he and Tim have talked everything through and they're fine.'

Dennis barrelled through the kitchen doors with a pot of coffee.

'Right, breakfast is underway. You two, tell me everything.'

Once Joyce and Ginger had finished running through everything they had discovered, concluded, assumed and checked, Dennis let out a big huff and crossed his arms over his chest.

'Well, I never. Love, eh? It's a bugger, that's for sure. I spend half my life keeping an eye out for the perfect match for our Ginger, and then sometimes, I think she's better off without.'

'I've told you before not to bother, but yes, it does often seem to be a lot of hard work and I'm not always convinced of the payoff.'

'Give over,' said Joyce. 'Even with… a certain number of marriages behind me, I've got plenty of time left for a few more.'

Dennis beamed. 'I do like your attitude, Joyce. Just make sure you have any future wedding parties here. I'll do you three for the price of two – plan ahead, you know.'

She laughed. 'Any excuse for a party. Maybe I can find triplets and as each one pops his clogs, I'll marry the next.'

This was all getting a bit off-track for Ginger's liking. Not only did they have to go and confront a killer, but Ginger needed to buy some new tights – every pair she had brought with her had a ladder in them. And then they needed to get ready for a party. But, before all that, she wanted more information from Dennis about the recent revelations.

'So, come on, then, we know Tim spoke to you last night. Is everything alright between you two?'

'Other than the fact that I wish he'd been honest with me from the beginning, yes, we're fine. I can understand his desire to move on. We all reinvent ourselves from time to time, and it really must have been a horrible time for him at such a formative period in his life. But as you can see, he's come through it all rather well. We have made a promise to be nothing but completely honest with one another from now on. He's also going to introduce me to his sister, who he keeps in touch with periodically, and he's going to reach out to his other siblings. He'd kept them at arm's length and was always finding excuses for me not to meet them, like they live overseas.'

'And do they?'

'If you count the Isle of Wight and Anglesey as overseas, yes.'

It sounded to Ginger as though there was quite a lot that Tim had kept from Dennis, and she just hoped that *everything* was out in the open now. She liked Tim, and over the last four years Dennis had been as happy as she had ever seen him. But they could talk about this further over a couple of martinis once this extremely busy day was done. She had a quick look in the coffee pot; it was empty.

'Right then, old girl, another cup of coffee before we go and catch ourselves a killer?' She gave Joyce a gentle shove.

'Oi, hands off, and don't "old girl" me.'

'You don't seem in too much of a rush.' Dennis gathered up their plates as Joyce replied.

'They're not going anywhere, and no one else is at risk. This was all about Caroline; there aren't any more targets for the killer's ire. Well, Ginger and I might be on their hit list once we've challenged them, but I'll add an extra weight to my handbag just in case.'

Ginger knew she wasn't joking.

The two women stepped out into a surprisingly bright and sunny Friday morning. It was still cold, but the kind of crisp cold with accompanying blue skies that made people feel happy and hopeful. Spring was peeking out from around a corner, waiting for an opportunity to reveal itself in all its glory.

For the first time, Ginger noticed the little green daffodil shoots starting to appear up on The Slopes behind St Ann's Well; the Pavilion Gardens were ready to wake up from winter. The array of greens had always been there, they had just been dulled by the grey skies of the last week. Then, Ginger's eyes had been drawn to the muddy puddles, but even they had dried up overnight. It was as though someone had turned a light on; the perfect day for Dennis to celebrate the next phase of The Lodge's history.

It seemed a shame to be heading inside and down into a basement, albeit a very attractive and calming basement with cucumber-infused water and the sort of music that usually made Ginger want to toss the CD player out of the window. She had to admit even that had rather grown on her during their last visit.

'Ready?' Joyce asked her as they reached the door of the spa.

'We're hardly leaving the trenches and heading over the top. Of course, I'm ready. Come on.'

55

They were greeted by the perky and perfectly made-up face of a young woman in a white coat. The smell of lavender wafted over to them and the gentle sound of flutes played from invisible hidden speakers.

'Hello, ladies, welcome. Do you have an appointment this morning?'

Joyce smiled. 'I'm afraid we don't. I realise that the chances are slim, but I was wondering if Lydia was in and had a gap in her diary?'

The young woman tapped a few keys on her computer keyboard.

'I'm so sorry; she is in, but her diary is full. Oh, no, there is an appointment at 3pm. Is that of any use?'

'Hello there?' Lydia appeared through a doorway with a mug in her hand, the string of a teabag hanging over the edge and steam rising from the bright red liquid. 'Were you hoping to see me?'

'I was, but it seems you're not free until three o'clock. Such a shame, but it is my own fault. You're on a break?'

'Yes, my next client arrives in ten minutes, so I'm just

sneaking in a quick zinger tea.' Lydia was all smiles. Either she had been on the receiving end of some pampering herself or life was treating her very well. Joyce glanced at Ginger, who was trying to peer at the computer.

'This is very cheeky of me, but would it be possible to have a quick chat? You see, I'd like to come more often and, rather than just booking a few things which look enjoyable, I thought it might be advisable to have a programme of sorts. Perhaps you could put that together for me?'

'Absolutely, take a seat.' Lydia started to walk towards the white sofa in the waiting area.

'Actually, do you have anywhere a little more... private?' Joyce tried to look embarrassed and pulled what she hoped was an amusing face.

'Oh... oh, of course. Come on through to my treatment room.'

'I'll wait here,' said Ginger as she flicked through some leaflets on the counter.

When the two women had entered the treatment room, Lydia sat on a stool that moved around on casters. Before she had a chance to say anything, Joyce jumped in.

'You look well; how are things with your gentleman friend? Good, I hope.'

The question clearly took Lydia by surprise.

'Fine. Yes, good, thank you. Now then, what are you hoping to achieve from your treatments? Once I know what you're looking for, it will be easy for me to put together a programme for you.'

'I am glad. It must be such a difficult situation, not being able to be together as often as you'd like. Which I assume would be all the time.'

'Err, yes. Now I can...'

'I have to confess, I've been involved with a number of married men. I always had high hopes that the situation might change and we could have a future together, but it was never meant to be.'

Joyce was listening for footsteps. She wasn't sure how long she could drag this out.

'That must have been very difficult, but we ought to…'

Just in time, Joyce heard the rattle of the door handle and Ginger walked in.

'Sorry to interrupt, I wanted to pass a message on to Joyce. You were absolutely right, dear, it was as you thought. I've made the phone call.'

She gave a cheery thumbs up and was about to retreat when Joyce stopped her.

'Stay, Ginger, grab a seat.'

'What's happening? I have a client in five minutes.' Lydia was glancing rapidly between them.

'I'm afraid you'll need to cancel it. We wanted to talk to you about last Saturday. Now, you told the police that you were with a client, but that's not true, is it?'

'I was, you can ask Sage. She's outside.'

'We'll come back to that. You must have been so excited once you heard that John's wife was divorcing him.'

'John? How do you know…?'

'You've given so much time, energy, emotion to that man. Leading a secret life just so you can be together, with no guarantee that would actually happen. But you were determined to stick by him, convinced that if you gave it time, he would make the right choice: you. He would choose you.'

'John and I were just waiting. Once his daughters were at university, he was going to leave his wife, but what business is this of yours?' Her eyes were darting between Joyce and Ginger. One minute she looked indignant, ready to turf them out; the next she was on edge. Joyce hoped this would play to their advantage.

'That's, what, a year or so away? Not long to wait, so it must have been particularly galling when he started spending so much time with Caroline.'

With that, Lydia's face slowly fell. The look she gave both women was stony and cold. She clearly knew where this was going.

'It turned out they had a lot to talk about, working closely on the Morton Hall proposal. Did they fall in love over the architectural plans? Did you have to listen to him talk endlessly about the latest fascinating titbit Caroline had discovered about the building's history? It must have got harder and harder, to know you were so close to having him for yourself after waiting patiently for so long, and now you were about to lose him to another woman just as you approached the finishing line.

'And then... then came the biggest blow. What you'd been waiting for actually happened. John received the divorce papers just as he was falling for Caroline. If only his wife had held off, you might have had time to regain John's attention. After he had managed to buy Morton Hall, he and Caroline might not have spent so much time together. Whatever happened, you needed more time and you didn't have it. You had to get rid of Caroline.'

The stony look cracked and Lydia smirked.

'Can you imagine waiting two years for someone? Putting your life on hold, sneaking around? He even came into the bar a couple of times with his wife. I had to endure all of that with a promise that it would be worthwhile. I'd made plans, *we'd* made plans, and that woman...

'We'd got to know her a little, and then of course she found out that John wanted to buy Morton Hall. They went from arguing about it to spending time planning its renovation. It took me a while to work out what was going on; he started off referring to her as *that bloody woman,* and then he was cancelling our dates to go to planning meetings with her. I saw what was happening. You'd have had to be blind not to.'

'He fell in love with her.' Joyce remembered the way John had run his fingers over the paperweight on his desk, the cast that

Caroline had given him. She remembered the resignation, the lack of spirit he'd shown last time they'd met.

'He was head over bloody heels.'

'And you needed to get rid of the competition.'

The smirk returned to Lydia's face. 'It was surprisingly easy to do, and yet miraculously, I was here when it happened. It seems it is possible to be in two places at once. As far as the police are concerned, I was here; they checked.'

Ginger stepped away from the door. It was her turn to speak.

'I'm sure they did, and yes, Thyme, Sage, whatever she's called, saw you come into work and will have confirmed that to the police. I imagine you chatted, made sure she and any other staff around saw you and registered your presence. Then you came in here, your treatment room. Only I've just checked on the computer while Thy... Sage made me a nice cup of tea in the back. Thank you, by the way, for choosing such a simple computer program, easy for a Luddite like me to work out. I checked and you didn't have any clients on Saturday morning, in fact you weren't due to work at all. You came in here, left by the fire exit...' Ginger nodded at the door in the far corner of the room '...and returned to the hotel. You'd left a fire door there ajar and let yourself in.

'You'd arranged to meet Caroline in the room that was dedicated to Mary, Queen of Scots. I assume you disguised your voice and used a different name when you phoned her, and it would have been easy enough to get her private phone number off John's mobile. You knew you wouldn't be disturbed; the only people going up there were carpenters and they'd most likely be busy in one of the other rooms. You could then dash back here, following the same route, pop out, say hello to your colleagues and return to the hotel.'

Lydia had listened to Ginger intently, and Joyce couldn't help but notice she had looked less and less sure of herself. Her plan wasn't foolproof; it was far too simple and she'd relied on the police taking Sage's statement as read and not checking the diary. They probably hadn't even been into her treatment room and spotted the fire exit. If Lydia hadn't been a suspect, they wouldn't have felt the need to dig beyond Sage's word. Lydia had even tried dropping breadcrumbs that led them to John, making it look like he had hated Caroline. A chance for revenge.

'This has been a pleasure, ladies, but all you have is my word against yours, and no one's going to believe a couple of confused, forgetful old women.'

'I'll confess to getting a bit forgetful,' Ginger admitted, 'but we have technology to help with all that.'

Joyce pulled her phone out of her pocket. She'd been recording the whole thing, although the thought of Ginger using technology to help with anything amused her no end.

'And that sounds like your next client.'

The heavy footsteps of more than one person were heading quickly towards the door of the treatment room. DS Harnby walked in without knocking.

'Oh good, you're all dressed. Now, can someone please explain why attending a health spa could be considered a police emergency?'

Ginger had opted for a loose dress that stopped just above the knees. Swirls of turquoise were set against a background of black. She wore with it an open knee-length silk shirt which repeated the pattern on the back, and accentuated her impressive barrage of a bust (her words). Turquoise teardrop earrings and black stilettos completed the outfit. She would be damned if Joyce was going to be the only one to have people staring at her outfit; she could match her pantone for pantone.

They'd been squirreled away in their own rooms and had come to the party separately, so she hadn't actually seen what Joyce was wearing. As Ginger entered the bar of The Lodge, a jazz band was playing a funky upbeat number. She felt good in her outfit and enjoyed seeing a couple of heads turn as she came through the door. Despite what others might think about her comfortable taste in clothing, she did enjoy dressing up.

The complimentary glances in her direction buoyed her. She was rather nervous; there was something she needed to do tonight and it had been on her mind for a long time. It never got easier, even after forty years. For now, however, she tried to distract herself and focus on the party.

The lights were very slightly dimmed, spotlights on the wall picking out Tim's artwork. Dennis was holding court at the bar. He wore his usual uniform of a navy pinstriped suit and his tie covered all the bases with stripes in three different shades of pink. The room was filled with the great and the good of Buxton's artistic scene; Ginger recognised the directors of the annual opera festival and book festival respectively. The Mayor of High Peak was in the corner wearing a dark suit with his chains of office glinting in the light as he stood in front of a painting.

Ginger headed for the bar, giving a few dance steps as she went. As Dennis caught her eye, she continued to dance the remaining few feet.

'Well, my darling, don't you look splendid?' Ginger spun to give him the full effect. He put his arms around her shoulders and turned her so a photographer could take a picture of them. 'We make rather a fabulous couple, don't you think?' he said, planting a kiss on her cheek. 'Where's Cagney?'

'I beg your pardon?'

'Well, she is the Cagney to your Lacey. Just don't ever carry guns; I dread to think about the carnage you two would leave in your wake with deadly weapons.'

'Oh, I don't know,' came a familiar voice over their shoulders, 'we'd probably shoot one another before we did any harm to innocent bystanders.' Ginger and Dennis spun round to see Joyce with her hand in the shape of a gun, pretending to blow the smoke off the tip. 'What does a girl need to do to get a drink around here?'

Dennis and Ginger simultaneously ran their eyes up and down the length of Joyce. She was wearing a very loud skirt, covered in prints of Marilyn Monroe's face. It was the fabric version of Andy Warhol's *Marilyn Diptych*, paired with a bright orange top, a gold cardigan and gold shoes. Her mountain of blonde hair was defying gravity in a pile that looked as if it was about to slip off the back of her head.

Ginger clapped. 'Joyce, you certainly bought into the artistic theme of the evening.'

'Don't ever expect me to do anything in a half-hearted manner.'

Dennis reached behind the bar for two coupe glasses of champagne and handed them to the women before reaching back for a third.

'To Cagney and Lacey,' he declared. The three clinked their glasses together. 'Thank you. I have no doubt the police would have found Caroline's killer in the end, but you made swift work of it, and now... well, there's been a noticeable feeling of peace around here since this morning. We can all close the door on a rather horrible event and instead focus on remembering Caroline.'

The conversation might have been held against a backdrop of music and partying, but briefly Ginger felt everything go still and quiet as the three of them remembered the woman who had been the focus of their lives for the last week. After another sip of champagne, Ginger broke the silence.

'Are the guests impressed with the new rooms?'

'Very, we've had a flurry of compliments all afternoon. Most of those checking in are regulars so it's rather like having family round to see your new home. It has been well worth all the hard work, dust and chaos.'

'Talking of dust, and those required to clean it up...' Joyce gave him a knowing look.

'Ah yes, about that.' Dennis took Joyce by the elbow and steered her, with Ginger following, to the far end of the bar where it was quieter. 'It was a dreadfully difficult decision and I'm afraid you might not agree, but I'm hoping you'll understand.'

KATE P ADAMS

'Don't tell me you've taken justice into your own hands and we've got another body in the hotel.'

'No, Joyce, although I did consider it, briefly. Helen will be resigning from her post over the weekend. Sunday is her last day.'

'Why didn't you tell the police?'

'My dear Ginger, I got close enough to pick up the phone, but I couldn't do it. It was Mr and Mrs Dalrymple, you see; if I tell the police about Helen, I have to tell the police about them. They are very elderly and have been part of The Lodge family for years; it would be like telling on... well, family. I just couldn't bring myself to do it. Of course, it might also be that Mrs Dalrymple needs help.'

Ginger took a quick look around the room. 'I notice they're not here.'

'No. Mr Dalrymple decided that it was best they went home. I have told him they can continue to return to The Lodge, but the first time something else goes missing, I will contact the police. He has agreed to that; not that he had much choice.'

'And Ed?'

'He will remain. Other than his rather fumbled attempt to sell a phone, which he only did because he was afraid for his mother's sake, he wasn't involved. He's a good lad.'

'Well, I must confess, I wasn't expecting that. It's very charitable of you,' said Ginger.

'It probably makes me party to a crime or whatever the technical term is, but it just feels like the right thing to do. I want to lay it all to rest. It's a new era for The Lodge.'

Something caught his eye and he smiled. Ginger turned and watched Tim as he spoke to the elderly man beside him.

'Who's that?' she asked, seeing that Joyce too was beaming.

'It's Frank,' Joyce replied, 'formidable Scrabble player and Tim's old art teacher.'

Ginger watched as Frank gave Tim a hearty pat on the back. They started to walk to another picture and Ginger could see the look of pride on the old man's face. Tim looked happy and relaxed. Something good had come out of all of this.

'Now, if you'll excuse me, ladies,' said Dennis, 'I need to circulate.'

'So should we,' declared Joyce as they watched him head towards the mayor. 'There must be an eligible bachelor around here – eligible and rich. We might find someone here for you, too.'

'About that.' Ginger looked into her champagne glass, not sure what she might find in there. Strength of some kind. She took a deep breath. 'You do realise that the person who broke my heart was a woman.'

'Yes, I do.'

'Oh.'

'Ginger dear, are you attempting to come out to me?'

'Well, yes.'

'That rainbow-flag-waving ship sailed a long time ago.'

'You knew?'

'Of course, I've always known.'

'But you haven't said anything.'

'It's not my place to. I knew you'd tell me when you were ready. Now, my glass is empty; let's get a top-up, and after that... well, maybe we can split up a couple.'

She grinned at Ginger, and then gave a wicked laugh as she led the way to the bar.

———

Join Joyce and Ginger for their next adventure in *Murder in the Wings* where they travel to London to drink cocktails, shop and solve a murder or two.

HAVE YOU READ THE CHARLETON HOUSE MYSTERIES?

Read the books that first featured Joyce Brocklehurst

Death by Dark Roast.

The annual Charleton House Food Festival is about to begin. But the first item on the menu is murder...

Nestled in the idyllic setting of Derbyshire's rolling hills, the ancestral home of the Fitzwilliam-Scott family seems an unlikely location for murder. But when a young man is bludgeoned to death with the portafilter of a coffee machine, recent thefts from local stately homes are put in the shade, and caffeine-loving café manager Sophie Lockwood finds her interest piqued by a pair of unusual cases.

Readers say:

'I absolutely adored this book!'

'The mysteries are fascinating and the writing is as elegant as Charleton House itself. A brilliant series I will read every word of.'

READ A FREE CHARLETON HOUSE MYSTERY

Building a relationship with my readers is one of the best things about writing. I occasionally send newsletters with details on new releases, special offers, interviews and articles relating to my books.

Sign up to my mailing list and you'll also receive the very first Charleton House Mystery, *A Stately Murder*.

Head to my website for your free copy and find out what happens when Sophie stumbles across the victim of the first murder Charleton House has ever known.

www.katepadams.com

ABOUT THE AUTHOR

After 25 years working in some of England's finest buildings, Kate P. Adams has turned to murder.

Kate grew up in Derbyshire, the setting for many of her books, and went on to work in theatres around the country, the Natural History Museum - London, the University of Oxford and Hampton Court Palace. Every day she explored darkened corridors and rooms full of history behind doors the public never get to enter. Kate spent years in these beautiful buildings listening to fantastic tales, wondering where the bodies were hidden, and hoping that she'd run into a ghost or two.

Kate has an unhealthy obsession with finding the perfect cup of coffee, enjoys a gin and tonic, and is managed by Pumpkin, a domineering tabby cat who is a little on the large side. Now that she lives in the USA, writing allows Kate to go home to her beloved Derbyshire every day, in her head at least.

www.katepadams.com

Printed in Great Britain
by Amazon

83751154R00150